To Ra

Thanks for being a great reader! Now, write your own stories down!

Frank

The Hardest Hit

A Sam the Hockey Player Novel

By

Frank Scalise

The Hardest Hit: A Sam the Hockey Player Novel

By Frank Scalise

Copyright 2011 Frank Scalise

Cover Design by Gordon Ennis

Back Cover photo by Aaron Noack
(used with permission)

ISBN 978-1463550059/1463550057

This book is for my son, Nico.

Fall.
Get up.
Fall.
Get up.

Hockey is life. Life is hockey.

Prologue

Sam was a born hockey player.

That's what my Dad always says, anyway. When I was real little, I believed it. It was exciting to think that I was actually born to do something I loved. Like it was destiny or something.

I'm eleven now, but I can't remember a time in my life that wasn't filled with the cold air and echoing sounds of a hockey rink. Skating was something I did as early as walking and it felt just as natural. By five years old, I was playing games in the Junior Mite division. Being on the ice felt more like home to me than the kitchen or living room of my house, or even my own room. And every time I stepped out on the ice, a tickle of excitement fluttered in my chest and made me smile for some reason that I couldn't quite explain.

Hockey was the greatest thing in my life. It was fun. It made my Mom, and especially my Dad, proud. My best friend Jill played with me and every year, almost every kid on my team ended up being my friend, too. We took road trips to Canada where we stayed in hotels with pools, so after the games were over we got to swim for hours. And every once in a while, I scored a big goal and we won the game.

It was perfect.

Then I turned eleven and went into the Pee-Wee division. That's when everything changed and my life was turned upside down.

1

"Summer sucks," I said.

"Yup," Jill agreed.

Jill's my best friend and has been forever. We met at learn-to-skate classes when we were three or four years old and started playing hockey together at five. She's been on my team every year. It's cool to have a friend you can talk to about anything.

The two of us sat on the curb in front of Jill's house, exhausted and sweaty from a round of street hockey. The hot August sun beat down on us. A tangled pile of hockey sticks and gloves lay on the ground off to the side. I moved my foot back and forth absent-mindedly listening to the rollerblade wheel scrape the pavement. Jill tore off her elbow pads and sighed heavily, wiping the sweat from her forehead and grinning a little. We didn't usually keep score. Instead, the rule was 'last goal wins.' Jill had just roofed one to the top of the net, so she was the winner for now.

"I mean it," I said. "I can't think of one good thing about summer."

"There's no school," Jill offered.

I furrowed my brow. She had a good point.

"And we get to go to the lake sometimes," she added.

"Okay," I relented. "There are a *couple* of good things about summer, but mostly it sucks." I didn't have to tell her why. Jill knew.

Summer meant no hockey.

Every year in late September, practices started. By October, we were playing games and the season lasted clear into April. The end of the season wasn't so bad, because there was almost always at least one weekend tournament sometime in May that we could play in, but once that ended, the hockey drought began. The NHL playoffs on TV helped take some of the sting out of it, but that was over by the first week of June, which left a long three months of no hockey.

"Summer sucks," I repeated.

"Yup," Jill agreed.

"You two are stupid," said a third voice from behind us.

I turned. Nate Bridger stood a few feet away astride his battered mountain bike. His closely cropped hair glistened with sweat. He squinted from the sun as he stared in our direction. He was a grade ahead of us in school. He'd always been bigger than me, but now I was surprised at how much he'd grown just since school let out. He had to be twice my size now. The way he threw his weight around on the ice last season was bad enough, but now he was a monster.

I swallowed and hoped he wasn't looking for trouble.

"Stupid?" I asked carefully. "What do you mean?"

Nate snorted. "Summer is the greatest invention in the world. There's no school."

"Yeah, I said that already," Jill said.

"Also," Nate said, "you get to go camping in the back yard, swimming at the pool and you can ride bikes all day long. There's no homework and you can stay up super late and then sleep in the next morning."

"Yeah," I said, "but—"

"There's barbeques," Nate continued, ignoring my interruption, "and baseball games at the sandlot that go on for way more than nine innings. Plus, on the Fourth of July, we get fireworks."

"Sure, fireworks are cool," I admitted, "but—"

"And it's warm out," Nate interrupted. "You don't have to wear hats or coats."

"That's true," Jill said.

"And that means not getting sick," Nate said.

"My cousin Drew got a bad cold last month," I said, hoping to poke a hole somewhere in Nate's theory.

"Did he get better?" Nate asked.

"Yeah."

"Well, if it would have been winter, he probably would've died or something."

I scowled. "That's a mean thing to say."

Nate snorted again. "Mean? I thought you were a hockey player."

"I am."

"Well, if you know anything about hockey, you know that you gotta be mean to play. And tough."

I pressed my lips together, considering. That wasn't what any of my coaches have ever said. My Dad, either.

Before I could answer, Jill spoke up. "Hockey is about skating and passing," she told Nate. "It's about playing together, as a team."

Nate shook his head and eyed the two of us. "Whatever," he finally said. "Maybe that's how they play in the girls league, but in Pee-Wee, there's body checking. It's real hockey, and you gotta be mean and tough." He jerked his thumb toward his chest. "Like me."

"Body-checking?" I asked. "I thought that didn't start until Bantams." Bantams started at thirteen, which seemed like about a century away right now.

"They check in Bantams, too," Nate said, "but we *start* in Pee-Wee." He squinted at me. "You didn't know that?"

I wasn't about to give Nate Bridger any satisfaction, so I answered, "Yeah, I knew. I just forgot, that's all."

He smiled. I don't know how he did it, but when Nate Bridger smiled, he looked even meaner than when he glared. "Well, don't 'forget' when you're on the ice, *Spam*. And keep your head up or you'll get your clock cleaned." He stood up on his pedal and pushed it forward, then turned around. "See ya, girls," he said over his shoulder as he rode away.

"Jerk," Jill muttered after him.

I shook my head. "That's one more thing I don't like about summer," I said. "Nate runs loose on his bike, riding around and shooting his mouth off for three months."

And calling me Spam, I thought. *Which I hate.*

"Yup," Jill agreed.

"He doesn't know anything, anyway," I said.

"Not much," Jill agreed.

"He's a stupid bully."

"Pretty much," Jill said. Then she crinkled her nose. "Well...he was probably right about the weather. Warm is nice."

I shrugged. "Yeah, okay. Probably."

"And the swimming," Jill added.

"Yeah."

"Fireworks, too."

Fireworks *were* cool, but I didn't feel like acknowledging that much of anything smart ever came out of Nate Bridger's mouth. So I changed the subject. "Well, he doesn't know anything about hockey, that's for sure."

"Not much."

I thought about body-checking and what Nate said about being mean. I had seen the pros check each other pretty hard, and sometimes they even got into fights. But youth hockey was nothing like that. Still, Nate seemed pretty sure of himself. "You don't think he's right about what he said, do you?" I asked Jill.

Jill took a deep breath and sighed. "Well, there is body checking in Pee-Wee. That's why I had to switch positions to goaltender this year."

"Really?" I asked, raising my eyebrows. "I thought you just wanted to wear all those cool pads."

Jill grinned a little. "That, too. But my Dad said that the boys were getting too big in Pee-Wee and that I might get hurt, being a girl." She scowled a little when she said this. I knew she didn't quite agree with what her Dad said.

"But you've been skating with boys since...well, you've always skated with boys. What's the big deal?"

She shrugged. "My Dad said that Pee-Wee is for eleven and twelve year olds, right? But he said some of the boys are *old* twelve year olds."

"What's that mean?"

"I guess it means that they turn thirteen during the season."

"Oh." I thought about it for a moment. The cutoff for each age level was the end of the year, but we played until April, so I guess it was possible. Some kids had to have birthdays in

January all the way up to the end of the season. "What's the big deal? That happens every year."

A bee buzzed by us and Jill took a mild whack at it with her street hockey stick. She missed but the bee got the hint and zipped away.

"All my Dad would say is that this is the age that changes really start happening and some boys at thirteen are going to be way, way bigger than me. Then he made me go talk to my Mom about it."

I cast a sidelong look at her. "Your Mom?"

Jill nodded. "She wanted to talk about other stuff."

"Other stuff?" I asked. Then I realized what she meant. "Uh-oh. You mean...?"

"Yup."

She didn't have to say it. I knew what she was talking about.

Puberty. The Change-o-rama. The big P. My Dad had "the talk" with me a few months ago. He didn't tell me anything I didn't already know from the school and from listening to other kids talk. Mostly, he hemmed and hawed and asked me if I understood. I said yes as quickly as I could to end the conversation.

Jill seemed pretty cool about the whole thing, though. I noticed she'd started looking more like a girl this last year, but I wasn't quite sure how I felt about it. I mean, sometimes I didn't like the idea, but sometimes I did. It was confusing. Sometimes it was easier just to ignore the whole thing.

I cleared my throat. "Uh, so that's why you changed to goaltender? So you wouldn't get hurt?"

Jill picked up a small piece of gravel next to the curb and chucked it at the nearby stop sign. *Ting.* As usual, she hit it dead center. "That's why my Dad *made* me change," she said.

I leaned back, resting my palms on the grass behind me. "Hunh," was all I could think to say. Jill was tougher than most boys in our class, though nothing like Nate Bridger. If she was worried about body checking, then maybe...

I shook my head at the thought. Jill wasn't worried. Her parents were. And parents always worried way, way too much about things like that.

I picked up a piece of gravel and threw it at the stop sign. My throw went wide and skittered harmlessly down the asphalt street.

"Nice shot, loser," Jill teased.

"Shut up," I said, getting to my feet. "C'mon, let's play. Shooting pucks isn't throwing gravel. Game on."

Jill smiled. "Okay."

Body checking, I thought as we put on our street gear.

It couldn't be that bad, could it?

I didn't know that the answer was – yes, it could.

2

"Skate hard between the blue lines," yelled Coach Valka, slapping the blade of his stick on the ice. "Come on, let's go!"

My legs felt like a pair of lead weights as I skated around the rink. Inside my helmet, the sound of my breath whooshed in and out. I coasted around the back of the net and glided up the boards, passing Jill in all of her goalie gear. She looked even more tired than me.

Coach Valka's stick rapped against the ice. He stood at the blue line against the boards, watching us approach. "Let's go, Parker!" he yelled at me. "You want to play center this year, you better show me you can skate!"

I lowered my head and pumped my legs as hard as I could, accelerating past him. Fire burned in my lungs, but I kept my eyes on the ice ahead of me until I crossed the far blue line. Relieved, I coasted down the boards and around the back of the opposite net.

Behind me, I heard Coach Valka barking at Jill. "Come on, goaltender. You're skating like you're towing an anchor. You think you don't have to skate because you're playing between the pipes? Think again!"

I rounded the turn and glided up the boards. The blue line always seemed to appear too quickly when we did this drill. Coach Andy, the assistant coach, stood at his blue line.

"Nice work, fellas," he called out as I approached with two other skaters I had caught up to. "Keep pushing."

I dug in and skated hard as soon as I hit the blue line again.

"Atta kid, Sam!" Coach Andy said from behind me. I heard his stick tapping on the ice. "Now catch him, boys!"

I smiled and my legs felt a little lighter. I didn't think there was anybody on the team that could catch me once I turned on the jets, but let them try.

A moment later, there was long, shrill whistle blast.

"Center ice!" Coach Valka ordered.

Grateful that the drill was over, I swung around and skated to the center of the rink. Coach Valka glided onto the face off dot and stopped hard. Little ice shavings flew up from his skates.

"Take a knee," he said. His voice still had the tinge of an accent, even though I knew he'd been in this country for a long time.

We all knelt down.

Coach Valka looked around at us. Then he said, "You're all breathing hard. That's good. There is a saying in hockey, 'the legs feed the wolf.' What does that mean?"

No one answered right away. We glanced around to see who might be the coach's first victim of the year.

Coach Valka waited a moment. Then he said, "Okay, so no one is into philosophy today. It means that every time we skate hard in practice it will pay off come game time. Why?"

Again, no one answered. After a few seconds, Coach Valka wordlessly pointed his gloved hand at his son, Spencer.

Spencer cleared his throat. "Uh, is it because we'll be in better shape than the other team, Dad...er, I mean, Coach?"

Coach Valka pressed his lips together and stared at Spencer.

Spencer squirmed.

"Are you asking me or telling me, son?" Coach Valka asked.

Spencer cleared his throat again. "Uh, it's because we'll be in better shape than the other team."

Coach Valka stared at him.

"Coach," Spencer quickly added.

Coach Valka stared a moment longer, then turned his gaze on the rest of us. "Is he right?"

We all murmured a tentative yes.

"Is he right?" Coach Valka asked again, raising his voice slightly.

"Yes!" we answered in unison.

Coach Valka nodded. "All right then. Good. So we skate hard in practice. *Every* practice."

I resisted the urge to groan. I thought that maybe practice was the Canadian word for torture.

"Now, some of you played for me last year in Squirts," Coach Valka continued. "You know what I expect. For those of you who are new to the team, you need to learn what I expect. The quickest way to find yourself on the bench or off the team is to not follow some very simple rules. Who knows those rules?"

No one spoke up.

Coach Valka pointed at Spencer again.

Spencer squirmed. "Uh, show up at practice?"

Coach Valka nodded, then pointed at me. "Sam?"

"Work hard," I said immediately. I knew it was the Coach's favorite rule.

"Good," he said. He turned to Jill. "Last rule?"

"Listen to our coaches," Jill replied without hesitation. We were both up on Coach Valka's rules. We'd seen some kids learn them the hard way. Getting benched stunk.

Coach Valka nodded. "And that is how simple it is," he said. He raised a finger and counted off the rules again. "Show up, work hard and listen to your coaches. Everyone got it?"

About half of the team let out a weak reply in sloppy cadence. "Yes, Coach."

Coach Valka scowled a little. "I couldn't quite hear that. Now, does everyone understand the rules of this team?"

"Yes, Coach!" we bellowed at the top of our lungs.

"All right, then." Coach Valka turned to Coach Andy. "Do you have anything for the team before we get started with body checking?"

Body checking? A sort of strange thrill went through me when he said that. I was excited, because body checking meant we were moving up a level in hockey. We weren't little kids anymore. But it was also a little scary, because I was pretty sure it was going to hurt. Maybe a lot.

I missed most of what Coach Andy said while I thought about body checking. Then I heard him say, "And the most important rule that I have is...?"

"Have fun!" most of the team screamed.

Coach Andy smiled. "Excellent."

"Now let's talk about body checking," Coach Valka said. "Why do we allow checking in hockey?"

No one answered.

Coach Valka waited.

Finally, Jake Runager put his hand up slowly.
"Jake?"

"To knock somebody down so they can't score a goal?"

Coach Valka shook his head. "No, not exactly."

"That's a good guess, though," Coach Andy told Jake.

"Anyone else?" Coach Valka asked.

No one answered.

After a few moments, Coach Valka said, "Andy?"

Coach Andy skated over near Coach Valka. Coach Valka dropped a puck and Coach Andy gathered it in with his stick.

"The reason we body check in hockey," Coach Valka told us, "is to knock a player off the puck." He lowered his shoulder and slowly slid into Coach Andy's chest, pushing him back. The puck remained where it was on the ice.

Coach Valka stopped pushing. He looked over his shoulder at us. "Now where's the puck?"

"Right there," several of us replied, pointing at the puck.

"And does Coach Andy have it anymore?"

"No," we answered in unison.

Coach Valka turned and glided back toward us. "That is why we body check. That is why you can only body check when a player has the puck or is near the puck." He reached out with his stick and pulled the puck toward him. "It is all about getting possession of the biscuit. Got it?"

We nodded.

"All right then. Now, there are a few important rules about body checking. Probably the most important is that you do NOT check someone from behind. Why is that?"

"You'll hurt them," Jill piped up.

"Exactly. It's dangerous and someone can get hurt." Coach Valka looked around at us. "It's a major penalty and could get you suspended from the league. And there's something else. Hitting someone from behind is cowardly. And we will not tolerate cowards on this team. Does everyone understand?"

"Yes, coach!"

"All right then," Coach Valka said. "Get up and let's practice some body checking."

We clambered to our feet. Coach Valka had us pair off and practice pushing against each other just like he'd done to Coach Andy earlier. I partnered with Spencer. Meanwhile, Jill and Coach Andy skated to the other end of the ice. Out of the corner of my eye, I saw him shooting pucks at her. Sometimes she dropped to her knees, and other times she stayed up. I had no idea why.

"Elbows in!" Coach Valka hollered. "Use your shoulder and drive from your hips."

We pushed each other back and forth for a while. It was actually kinda fun, like tug of war in reverse. Spencer was taller than me but I think I was stronger because I had an easier time pushing him back than he did pushing me. Or maybe he just wasn't trying.

When we'd finished the pushing drill, Coach Valka lined us up near the boards about four feet apart. He started at one end of the line and skated along the boards in front of Jake.

"Hit me," he told Jake.

Jake stood stock-still, frozen. I knew what he was thinking. Hit the coach? No way. He'd probably tear your head off or something.

"It's all right," Coach Valka said. "Just lay a body check on me."

Jake hesitated. Then he tried to put his shoulder up against Coach Valka's chest. His shoulder only reached Coach's belly. I didn't think my shoulder would reach much higher, and my turn was coming.

Jake pushed.

Coach Valka stood his ground, unmoving.

Jake stopped and backed up. He looked around at all of us, a little confused and unsure of what to do next.

"Instead of just pushing me this time," Coach Valka said, "I want you to skate into me. Drive that shoulder in just like before."

Jake hesitated again, but finally took a strong stride and drove his shoulder into Coach Valka's stomach again. This time, Coach Valka slid into the boards, making a crashing noise as his body hit against the glass.

Some of us jumped, and a murmur of surprise, excitement and a little bit of fear ran up and down the line. I winced a little myself – it looked like it hurt.

Coach Valka seemed to read my mind. "Who thinks that hurt?"

After a moment, a few of us raised our hands.

Coach Valka waited.

After another moment, pretty much everybody's hand was in the air.

"All right then," he said. "That's what I would expect. It *does* look like it hurts, doesn't it?"

"Yeah," I muttered. "It does."

"The truth is," Coach Valka said, "that sometimes it does. But most of the time, not very much. Especially if you know how to take a check."

He glided down the boards, looking at each of us as he spoke.

"You take a check the same way you receive a pass," he said, dropping the blade of his stick onto the ice. "You don't keep your stick rigid and let the puck hit it, do you? No. If you do that, the puck bounces off your stick. Instead, you *accept* the pass." He mimed moving his stick back slightly as an imaginary puck arrived. "You cradle it. Who remembers when we passed raw eggs back and forth last season?"

I raised my hand, along with several others. That had been fun, especially when Spencer broke his and spilled yolk all over the ice.

"That drill was to teach you to accept a pass gently, with soft hands," Coach Valka said. "You do the same thing with a body check. Don't fight it. Relax. Go with it. *Accept* the hit."

I frowned. Letting someone hit you didn't sound like a great plan to me.

"This drill," Coach Valka said, "is called The Gauntlet." He pointed to Jake. "Jake, you start. Come down the line and take a check from each player. Remember to accept the hit. Let the boards absorb the force of it."

Jake skated tentatively in front of a kid I didn't know yet wearing a Detroit Red Wings jersey. I figured he was probably a second year player and already knew how to check. When he powered his shoulder into Jake and slammed his body into the boards, I figured I had guessed right.

The glass shook and quivered from the force of the collision. I expected Jake to be squished to a pulp, but when the Red Wings kid backed up, there was Jake, still standing.

"Did that look like it hurt?" Coach Valka asked.

"Yes!" said the whole team with certainty.

Coach Valka turned to Jake. "Jake, did that hurt?"

Jake shook his head. "Not really. I mean, a little, but not really."

"All right then," said Coach Valka. "Let's work The Gauntlet."

Jake continued down the line. When he got to me, I skated into him and plastered him against the boards. He absorbed the check with a grunt and moved on.

One by one, we took turns running the gauntlet. When my turn came, my mouth was dry and I could feel my heart pounding in my chest. Spencer was the first one to check me and he pushed me into the boards with very little force.

"Stop!" Coach Valka said, blowing a short burst on his whistle. He pointed at Spencer. "No lame checks, Spence. We work hard in practice. We don't take it easy on each other."

"Yes, sir," Spencer said, hanging his head a little.

"And you need to loosen up, Parker," he told me. "You're too tense. You can't take the check that way. If Spencer had laid an actual check on you, you'd have gotten hurt."

"Yes, coach," I answered.

Coach Valka blew his whistle again and motioned for the drill to continue.

I took check after check. Each collision rattled my teeth, making me glad for my mouthguard. The force from the initial contact jarred me and hurt a little, but Jake had been right. It wasn't much. By the third or fourth time, I started to relax and it hurt even less. In fact, a couple didn't hurt at all. By the time I reached the end of the gauntlet, I was starting to understand what Coach Valka meant about accepting the check.

We worked the Gauntlet for a long time. I had the chance to check a bunch of times and went down the line myself twice more. When we finally broke up for passing and shooting drills, I felt pretty good about the whole body checking thing.

In fact, I felt like there wasn't much that could knock me down.

Boy, was I wrong.

3

Dad was late picking me up after practice.

I stood out in front of the rink with my bag over my shoulder and my sticks in my hand. I always took two sticks to practice or games in case one of them broke. I only learned how to do a slapshot last year in Squirts and even though it isn't as powerful as you'll see in the pros or at a Chiefs game, I can sometimes crank it. Of course, you always run the risk of snapping a twig when you do that. Secretly, I kinda hoped it would happen in the middle of a game. Everyone would see the stick break from the force of my slapshot. They'd have to think it was pretty powerful, and pretty cool.

I was day-dreaming about blasting a shot from the blue line right over the goalie's shoulder, just like Stevie Y did against St. Louis in the playoffs one year, when Dad pulled up in his Saab. He rolled to a stop in front of me. He didn't bother getting out. Instead, I heard the metallic click of the hatchback popping open.

I tossed my bag into the back of the car and slid the sticks over the top of the back seat and wedged the blades underneath the passenger seat.

"Watch the roof," Dad said. His voice sounded a little funny. I guessed he was extra tired or something.

"Got it," I said, then slammed the hatchback.

As I slid into the passenger seat and buckled my seatbelt, I cast a sidelong glance at Dad. He stared out the windshield with a strange look on his face. I couldn't decide what the look meant. I just knew that it seemed...well, kinda empty.

Dad put the car in gear and drove toward home. We were both silent for a little while. Dad usually had the radio on, listening to the oldies station, but today it was just the digital clock display and no music.

Both of my parents are teachers. Dad teaches history and Mom teaches math. I don't know what might make a person tired or whatever from talking about history, unless maybe even the history teachers get bored to death with all those names and places, but sometimes my Mom and Dad both seem really worn out. Especially lately.

I tried to start a conversation with Dad. "We learned how to body check today," I said.

"Hmmmm," he grunted.

"It didn't hurt," I said, lying just a little.

"Hunh," Dad grunted. Then he glanced over and cleared his throat. "Coach got you playing center again?"

I shrugged. "We didn't do any positional drills, just the body checking mostly."

Dad grunted again and turned back to the road.

"The body checking didn't really hurt, though," I said.

He didn't answer.

I turned away and watched the houses and yards glide by. If Dad didn't want to talk, fine. It was just strange, was all. Usually, he was at practice for at least part of the time. Even when he missed, he still always seemed to have some suggestion about how I could do better.

We pulled into the driveway. I expected Dad to push the remote button for the garage door, but he just sat in the driveway, idling the motor. After a minute, he said, "You go on in. I've got some work to do at the school."

I shrugged. Whatever.

I pulled my gear and sticks from the back of the car. Dad pulled away without waving goodbye.

Weird.

I went into the house. Usually by this time, the smell of dinner would fill the place, but I couldn't smell anything other than the hockey stink from my hands and the bag over my shoulder.

"Mom?"

I dropped the bag in the entry way and leaned my sticks in the corner.

"Mom?" I called, a little louder.

"In here," she answered from the kitchen in a strange voice.

I walked into the kitchen. She'd been sitting at the kitchen table, but stood as I entered. I saw her wipe at her eyes before she flashed me a tired smile. "Did you have a good day at school?"

My eyes narrowed in concern. My Mom wasn't a crier. If she was upset enough to be crying, then...all of the sudden, a horrible thought occurred to me.

"Did Grandpa die?" I asked, fear rising in my chest.

Mom's eyes widen in surprise. "No! Why would you ask that?"

"You're crying," I said. "And Dad was acting weird in the car."

Mom was quiet for a moment, as if she were considering something. Then she said, "Everything's fine, Sam. How was school?"

"Fine," I answered.

"Hockey practice?"

"Good," I said. Then I added, "We started body checking today."

Her eyes widened in concern. "Really? Isn't that dangerous?"

I shook my head. "Coach says not if you check right and if the other guy keeps his head up."

She pursed her lips. "Is that something you have to do? Check, I mean?"

I shrugged. "I think so."

"It sounds dangerous."

"Mom —"

"I don't remember reading about this in the paperwork they sent home."

"It was," I said, though I wasn't sure. "But Mom —"

"I just don't want you to get hurt."

"Mom —"

"Is there a league where they don't check?"

I felt a little bit of anger tickle my chest. "Yeah. Baby leagues."

She stopped and gave me an appraising look. I could tell I was at a crossroads. Either the conversation was going to be over or I was in for a one-way lecture, *a la* Mom. I held her gaze, trying not to appear like I was challenging her to the lecture.

She sighed. "I guess it's one of those things," she said.

"What things?"

"Things about men and hockey that I don't get and never will," she told me. Then she waved a dismissive hand. "Now, what do you want for dinner?"

"Anything but mac and cheese," I said. "I'm sick of mac and cheese."

"There was a time when you could eat that seven days a week," she said, moving to the fridge and opening the door.

"That's probably why I'm sick of it," I offered. "Is there pizza?"

She removed a mini-pizza from the freezer. "Pizza," she announced. "The new mac and cheese." She waved me away with the box. "Now go shower. You stink like a hockey player."

"I *am* a hockey player," I said with a smile, and headed off to take a shower.

4

I ate my pizza in front of the television, watching the cartoon channel. I didn't like most of the old cartoons that were on when my parents were kids, but there were a couple of good ones. Right now, an episode of Tom and Jerry was on. The silly cat was chasing the mouse around with a hammer, but no matter how fast he swung it, the mouse moved and he couldn't hit him. Then he got the cat to swing and miss, just in time to hit a trampoline. The rebound pounded the cat into the grass up to his shoulders.

I smiled. Cartoons never got old.

While I was eating, the door opened. I looked up to see my Dad walking in. He hung up his coat and gave me a distracted wave. Then he disappeared upstairs.

I went back to the cartoons and my pizza. When I'd finished, I took the plate into the kitchen. Mom and Dad suddenly appeared in the doorway.

Dad's expression was still a little vacant. Mom had a forced smile on her face.

Something weird was going on.

I wondered for a minute if maybe Grandpa really did die. Maybe Mom was just afraid to tell me about it. Or maybe I was in trouble. I racked my brain to think of anything I'd done that I'd get in trouble for, but I couldn't think of anything recent. Then I figured that maybe it wasn't something that I did. Maybe we were moving away or something.

"Hey, Mom. Hey, Dad. Er...what's up?"

Mom opened her mouth to speak, then closed it. She glanced at Dad. Dad let out a small sigh and motioned to the kitchen table. "Have a seat, Sam," he said.

Uh-oh. I swallowed. The kitchen table was for meals. Any other kind of talk at the kitchen table was bound to be a serious one.

I sat down and both of my parents did, too. We were all silent for a few seconds, then my Dad sighed again. "Sam, your mother and I have something to tell you."

"Is it bad?"

Dad didn't answer right away. Then he said, "Well, it's not good. But we want you to know that it has nothing to do with you."

"Okay." I paused. "Then why are you telling me?"

Dad gave me a confused look. "Huh?"

"Well," I explained, "if it doesn't have anything to do with me, then I'm just wondering why you're telling me about it."

"What your father means," Mom said, "is that it affects you, but it isn't your *fault*. You aren't part of the reason."

I shook my head, confused. "Reason for what?"

Mom and Dad looked at each other, then back at me.

"Sam—," Mom began.

"Your mother and I are getting a divorce," Dad finished.

I stared at both of them.

A divorce.

That couldn't be. That was something that happened to other kids in other families. Not to us.

"Sam?" Mom asked. "Did you hear your father?"

I nodded dumbly.

Divorced.

"Do you have any questions?" Dad asked.

Questions? Are you kidding? I had a million of them.

Why are you getting divorced? What did I do?

When was this happening?

Who was I going to live with? When would I see whoever I didn't live with?

Do we have to move?

What about my hockey team?

What did I do to cause this?

"Sam?" Dad asked. Both of my parents were leaning forward slightly, watching me carefully. "Are you all right?"

I nodded my head. "I'm fine."

"I know this is a surprise to you," Dad said, "But—"

"I'm not surprised," I fibbed, without thinking. "I saw it coming."

Dad raised an eyebrow. "You did?"

I took a deep breath and nodded. "Yeah. It was pretty obvious."

Mom and Dad exchanged an unreadable look. When they both looked back at me, I could see that one or both of them was going to ask me some more questions. That was the last thing I wanted, so I said, "Is that all? Because I'm really pretty tired from practice, so I was thinking I'd go to bed."

Neither one of them spoke. Finally, my Dad let out another one of those small sighs and said, "Sure, champ. Go ahead."

I gave them a weak smile like the one my Mom had come in with, got up and left the kitchen. On my way up the stairs, all I could think about was how that was the last time I'd ever be able to think of them as "Mom and Dad."

Upstairs in my room, I asked myself all of the same questions I'd had in the kitchen, but there weren't any answers. I told myself that only babies cried into their pillow. I guess I was wrong, though, because I filled mine with tears before I finally fell asleep.

5

"Divorced?!" Jill gaped at me. "You're kidding!"

I shook my head glumly. "I wish I was."

Jill bit her lower lip. She always did that when she was thinking. I looked around the locker room to see if any of the other players had heard us, but no one was paying attention. They were all at various stages of getting on hockey gear for our first game. Jill sat next to me, fully dressed. She got her gear on in the women's locker room and joined us after all of the boys were dressed enough for her to be in with us.

"Why?" she finally asked.

"I don't know."

She looked at me closely. "Have they been fighting a lot lately?"

I shook my head.

"Because when Kayla Schaefer's parents got divorced, she said that she heard them yelling a lot right before."

I reached down to my skate and untied it. Then I started re-tying it. I regretted telling Jill about the divorce already. I should have waited until after the game or some other time when we were just hanging out. But I couldn't help it. The whole thing was burning a hole in my chest, and she was the only one I could tell.

"What else did Kayla say?" I asked, glancing up at her.

"Like what?"

"Like, who does she live with?"

"Her Mom," Jill said. "Who do you think you'll live with?"

I swallowed. I didn't want to have to think about that. "I don't know," I said. Then I asked, "Did her parents say why they got divorced?"

Jill shook her head. Then she leaned forward and lowered her voice. "Kayla said she thought it was her fault, though."

My stomach lurched. I tried to act nonchalant. "Why'd she think that?"

"She'd been getting into a lot of trouble, I guess," Jill said. "She figured that her parents just didn't want to deal with it, so they got divorced instead."

I swallowed over the lump in my throat. "What kind of trouble did she get into?"

Jill glanced around the room, then back at me. "Boys," she whispered.

I raised my eyebrows. "Like how?"

Jill shrugged again. "She wouldn't say. She just said it was bad enough to make her parents get divorced."

I thought about that for a minute. I couldn't think of anything I had done that was even close to what Kayla Schaefer was talking about, whatever that was. So I was safe there. But maybe it wasn't just one single thing. Maybe it was just me over all.

That made me think even harder. If it was one thing, I could change that. But how was I supposed to change *everything*?

I finished tying my skate and sat back up.

Jill eyed me carefully. "You didn't do anything really bad, did you?"

I shook my head.

"Well, then it must not be your fault," she concluded, and offered me a smile.

"Maybe not," I said, "but no matter whose fault it is, I don't want it to happen at all."

She nodded sympathetically. "Yeah, it definitely sucks." Then her face brightened and she looked up. "Hey, maybe they'll change their minds!"

I looked over at her quizzically. "You mean stay married?"

"Yeah, exactly." She bobbed her head up and down with excitement. "Maybe they'll decide getting a divorce is a bad idea after all."

"And stay married?" I repeated.

"Exactly." She smiled, and reached out and slapped me on the shoulder.

I nodded my head, thinking. She could be right. It could happen. Maybe they would find some reason to forget about getting a divorce. Maybe they'd change their minds.

And maybe I could help make that change happen.

Coach Valka gave us a quick pep talk before the game. Then Jill led us out onto the ice. I walked in line behind my teammates, ideas zipping through my head. What if I got straight A's in school? Or won some kind of an award? Would that work?

As I took warm-up laps around the ice, I searched the stands for my parents. On the second lap, I spotted them. They were sitting together, which I took as a good sign. I waved and waved like a junior mite until Mom spotted me and waved back.

Coach Andy dumped out the pucks for warm up. I gathered one onto my stick and skated along, stick-handling the puck back and forth. That's when it occurred to me.

Hockey.

That's how I'd keep my parents together.

I'd be a star. I score a hundred goals or something like that. They'd be so proud of me that they would have to stay married.

I ripped a shot into the top corner of the net and skated around the back, smiling. It might just work.

6

Warm ups ended and we collected the pucks and sent them skittering over toward our bench. At the far end of the ice, the other team did the same. We gathered at the bench. Coach Valka barked out the starting lines.

"Parker, you take center and start your line," he said.

I smiled and nodded. Being a starter was a good way to get things going. "Yes, Coach!"

He reached out with his notepad and tapped me on the helmet. "Let's jump all over these guys early," he said. "Get off to a good start."

"Yes, sir!" I said.

I turned and skated to center ice, glancing up in the stands for my parents. Both sets of eyes were on me. I felt my heart race as I glided toward the face-off dot. I was staring down at the red dot, thinking about what I had to do, when a sneering voice broke into my thoughts.

"Well, look at this, will ya?"

I glanced up. Nate Bridger glared at me through the bars of his facemask.

"Hello, *Spam*," he crooned. "You ready to get crunched?"

I gave him my best stare and lowered my stick to the face-off dot. "You've got to catch me first, Nate."

He slapped his stick blade down onto the ice opposite mine. "No worries there. In hockey, there's no running out of bounds."

The referee skated to a stop, puck in hand. He checked with Jill to see if she was ready, then with the opposing goaltender. Nate whacked at my stick with his while the ref checked with the timekeeper. Then, without warning, he dropped the puck and the game was on.

Nate didn't even go for the puck. Instead, he plowed directly into my chest with his shoulder. It felt a lot like the hits I took in practice, only a little harder. I tried to go with it and absorb the force of the check. Nate was a lot bigger than me, though. I ended up falling over backwards and landing in a heap.

Nate took a moment to stand over the top of me. He smiled sarcastically and said, "Get used to that, Spam. That's how it's going to be every shift."

Then he skated after the play.

I scrambled to my feet. A quick glance toward my parents told me that they'd seen everything. That wasn't exactly the beginning I was hoping for.

Nate's team was called "The Ducks," probably named for the Anaheim Ducks. Their jerseys were a dark green. When I went after the puck, it seemed like there were about twelve of the dark green jerseys buzzing around the ice. They passed the puck pretty good, especially for this early in the season. Usually it took a few games for kids to get used to each other.

I swallowed hard and skated into position. Nate was kind of a puck hog, so I spent a lot of time playing him defensively. He tried to stick-handle past me with some fancy move, but I poked at the puck with my stick and knocked it away from him.

"Hey!" Nate yelled.

One of my wingers took possession of the loose puck and skated toward the Ducks' zone.

"Dump and change!" Coach Valka hollered from the bench as we crossed the center ice red line.

Obediently, the winger flipped the puck deep into the offensive zone and all three of us skated to the bench. The second line poured onto the ice as we left it.

"Nice poke-check, Sam," Coach Andy said from the far end of the bench as he managed the defensemen and their line changes.

I nodded and said thanks, but I was thinking, *Way to get dumped on your butt, Parker.*

As if he could read my mind, Coach Valka put his hand on my shoulder. "Try to bear down and win those face-offs, Parker," he said. "We can't score if we don't have the puck."

I nodded and replied, "Yes, Coach."

He gave my shoulder a squeeze and moved off, hollering at one of the wingers to cover the point in our defensive zone. I sneaked a glance over to where my parents were sitting, but it was impossible to see them from where I sat.

Good.

I took a deep breath and regrouped. I'd been playing hockey all my life. I knew how to react to different situations. All it took was a little bit of strategy. All I had to do was put my mind to it and figure out how to beat them.

The Ducks were good passers, but Nate was a puck hog and didn't pass. I was faster than Nate. So if I could poke check the puck away from him again, I might have enough open ice to skate it up. Maybe even get a shot on goal.

"Change, change!" Coach Valka yelled.

The second line came to the bench. As soon as Carson, the other center, reached the door, I hopped onto the ice and skated hard into the play. The other center dumped the puck softly into our zone and went to the bench for their change. Out of the corner of my eye, I saw Nate step onto the ice and make a bee-line for me.

I ignored him and skated after the puck. Our defenseman saw me coming with speed, so he moved aside. I gathered up the puck on my stick and swooped behind our own net.

"Go, go, go!" Jill yelled at me. "Open ice!"

I pushed the puck in front of me, skating as fast as I could. Nate changed direction to adjust for my move behind the net, but I could see he had no chance of catching me. The two opposing wingers stayed with their man, so I had a clear space right up the middle of the ice. Way ahead of me, I saw the Ducks defensemen skating backwards to defend their zone. In the process, they were giving up the entire neutral zone, something Coach Valka would have never allowed our 'D' to do.

Taking advantage of Nate lagging behind, I jetted toward the Ducks' blue line. Just inside the blue line, both defensemen slowed up. I faked moving to my left, then to my right. One of the 'D' bit on the fake, but the other changed direction and came toward me.

I kept up my speed and shot right between the two 'D,' leaving no one between the goaltender and me.

My heart was racing from skating hard up the ice and now it kicked into overdrive. I saw the goalie crouch and prepare for my shot. Without slowing down, I wristed it at the space between his pads. The puck leapt off my stick like a shot and zipped through the goaltender's legs. The back of the net plumed outward. The red light came on. The ref blew his whistle and pointed at the net. The crowd erupted in a cheer.

Goal!

I raised my hands in the air in celebration. Exhilaration blasted through me. I let out a whoop. Then I looked over at my parents. Both were beaming and clapping for me.

Maybe my plan would work after all.

My teammates gathered around and congratulated me as we skated back to center ice for the face-off following a goal. I saw the scoreboard flip from a '0' to a '1' for the home team. I couldn't help grinning. Nothing felt as good as scoring a goal.

At the face-off, Nate seethed with anger. "Lucky shot, Spam," he said.

I ignored him and put my stick onto the face-off dot.

"Keep your head up, hot shot," Nate growled.

7

My goal really got our team fired up. Now it seemed like we were the ones buzzing around the ice and making great passes instead of the Ducks. On the other side of the ice, the Ducks seemed to struggle all of the sudden. They tried to force passes that weren't safe. Several other players started to do a Nate imitation and keep the puck to themselves. Coach Valka had taught us to play a tough game defensively, so none of those attempts worked out for them.

Mid-way through the second period, Carson took a pass right in the slot from one of the wingers. He fired the puck on net. It seemed to pinball off of a couple of players in front of the goaltender before ricocheting into the back of the net.

The red light came on again and everyone on the bench banged their sticks and the crowd cheered.

2-0.

On my next shift, I could tell the Ducks were getting angry. More than that, I could tell Nate was getting furious. Every time I met his gaze, he glared at me. Every chance he got, he slammed into me. On every face-off, he drove his shoulder into me, but I was getting better at absorbing the hit. A couple of times, I slipped to the side, causing him to slide right past with barely a rub against me. Both times, I took possession of the puck and started up ice with it.

"It's a speed game," Coach Valka said in between the second and third period. "We're faster than they are, boys. Let's use our speed."

Across the ice, I could hear the other coach yelling at the Ducks players. I couldn't make out the words, but the tone was unmistakable – "You've got to do better!"

When the third period started, the Ducks came at us hard. For a while, their energy put us back on our heels and it seemed like the tide might turn. Then I caught Nate coming across center ice with his head down. I glided into him, planting my shoulder into his chest in a perfect open ice hit. The force of the blow, and probably the surprise, knocked him off the puck. He flailed his arms and avoided falling down. That didn't stop me from scooping up the puck and skating in all alone on the goaltender.

I fired the puck at the five-hole again, but this time the goalie slammed his pads together. The puck rebounded off his legs right back to me. I took control of the puck, moved it onto my backhand and shoveled toward the net. The goalie slid across and flailed at the puck as it flew past him and into the net.

Goal!

I pumped my fist three times. Before my teammates could congratulate me, I looked for my parents. They were standing and clapping with enthusiasm. Their faces were bright and their eyes were shining. My Mom leaned over and said something to my Dad. He smiled and nodded at whatever she said.

I grinned.

I was a genius. My plan was going to work.

When I skated into position for the faceoff, I could almost see the anger coming off of Nate in red waves. He didn't bother to say anything to me, but only glared. When the ref dropped the puck, he charged forward. I slipped to the side, then skated after the puck.

"Change!" Coach Valka shouted.

When I reached the puck, I flicked it into the corner of their zone and turned toward the bench. Suddenly, I felt a sharp, heavy stinging on my calf. My leg buckled and I fell to my knees.

The ref blew his whistle. "Slashing!" he yelled. "Twenty-Two Green. Get in the box!"

I looked over my shoulder. Nate Bridger skated away from me toward the Ducks penalty box. I realized what had happened. He'd swung his stick at me and hit me in the back of the leg. There was no padding on the calf area, and his hit hurt bad.

I guessed that since Nate couldn't catch me, he'd decided to start playing dirty. Luckily, the ref saw him do it, so he got a penalty.

I rose to my feet and skated gingerly to the bench, testing out the right leg. Shock waves of pain shot up and down my leg. The source of the waves was a knot that felt like it was the size of my fist.

Limping, I left the ice and took a seat on the bench. As much as my leg hurt, I wondered if it was badly injured. My big plan to keep my parents together wouldn't work if I could never skate again.

Instantly, Coach Andy was in front of me. He was some sort of a doctor in real life, so he always took care of us if we got hurt. His warm hands found the center of the huge knot in my calf and started kneading the muscle. That hurt, too, but it also made it feel better.

"Cheap shot, huh?" Coach Andy said while his fingers dug into my calf.

"Uh-huh," I managed, gritting my teeth.

"The ref should have given him a major penalty instead of a minor," Coach Andy said. "That was clearly intent to injure."

"Uh-huh," I agreed, my jaw still clenched.

"Feels like it'll be nothing more than a bruise," Coach Andy told me. "We'll try to get you back out for your next shift, but if it hurts too much, you tell me. Okay?"

"Okay," I grunted.

Coach Valka yelled at the referee about the call being a minor penalty and not a major, but the argument fell on deaf ears. In hockey, you're never really arguing for the call that just occurred because the refs are rarely, if ever, going to change the call. What you're arguing for is the next call. And Coach Valka was great at arguing for that next call.

"He just about severed my kid's leg!" he hollered at the referee.

I nodded in agreement. It sure felt like that.

"He was going for the puck," the ref told Coach Valka.

"What puck?" Coach Valka argued. "The puck was somewhere up in British Columbia when he slashed my player!"

"That's not what I saw," said the ref.

"I don't care what you saw," Coach Valka said, "I'm telling you what happened."

The ref skated to a stop in front of our bench. In an even voice, he asked, "Would you like a bench minor for unsportsmanlike conduct, coach?"

Coach Valka said nothing. After a moment, the ref skated away.

"Going for the puck," Coach Valka muttered, shaking his head. "Get your eyes checked." Then he motioned to Carson. "You're up. Let's make them pay on the scoreboard."

I tried to watch the play as our team lined up for a power play opportunity. With Nate in the box, the Ducks were only allowed four players on the ice to our five. I hoped we'd be able to take advantage of the situation. But Coach Andy kept working on my leg for almost two straight minutes, so I missed whoever took whatever shot that went in. I heard the cry of the crowd on our side and the groans across the ice. Coach Andy glanced over his shoulder, then returned to my leg.

"Feel any better?" he asked.

I nodded. It was still sore, but the waves of pain were more like small ripples now. Coach Andy smiled and tapped me on the helmet.

"You up, Parker?" Coach Valka asked.

"Yes, Coach," I said in the strongest voice I could muster.

I skated out for the face-off. My leg felt a little bit like a loose rubber band, but it didn't hurt as much. I tried not to show any pain or effect as I skated.

Nate was waiting for me at center ice. "Have a nice fall?" he asked, his voice full of sarcasm.

"Have a nice trip to the box?" I retorted.

He shrugged. "Who cares? This game is over for us. As far as I'm concerned, the rest of this period is about pain. Yours."

I didn't have a reply for that. Thankfully, the ref skated to the dot and dropped the puck, so I didn't have to say anything.

Nate tried to drill me right off the face-off again. I pushed to the side, but the pain in my leg from the effort slowed me down a little bit. He caught me pretty good in the chest. I toppled to the ice in a replay of what had happened at the beginning of the game.

"Ha!" Nate shouted, and skated off.

I got back to my feet and back into the play.

Things got a little chippy from there. It seemed like every player on the Ducks felt the same way about the game as Nate did. They didn't exactly quit trying to score, but if it came down to a choice between taking a shot or giving a hit, most of them were choosing the hit.

With seven minutes left, Gabe, who played defense, slid down the bench to sit behind me. "Why aren't you going for the hat trick, Sam?" he asked.

"Huh?"

"You've got two goals, right?"

"Yeah."

"So one more is the hat trick. That'd be pretty cool, getting a hat trick in the first game of the season."

I nodded like it wasn't the coolest thing in the world, but once I started thinking about it, I couldn't get it out of my head. Both Mom and Dad seemed excited by my first goal. They'd been *really* excited when I got the second one. Getting a hat trick might make them realize I was a bona fide star player. And that might make the difference.

I took a deep breath and decided. I had to go for it.

On my next shift, I watched for any opportunity to break out. With all of the Ducks trying extra hard for hits, I figured there had to be a chance.

Late in my shift, the Ducks dumped the puck in and went for a change. I skated hard after the puck. The pain in my calf nagged at me, messing with my stride and causing me to have something similar to a slight limp. I heard Coach Valka calling for a line change, too, but I was getting close to the puck, so I kept going.

The dump-in shot from the Ducks player had been a weak one. The puck dribbled to a near stop along the boards. I gathered it in with my stick and started to turn up ice with it. The ice was a little rough with all the grooves from hard skating. The puck caught on one of those grooves and hopped off my stick. I stopped, reversed direction and got control of it again. Then I started back the other direction.

That was when the world slowed down.

I didn't see what hit me, though I imagined it must have been someone about eight feet tall and around seven hundred pounds. The force of the blow felt like a giant staple in my chest. All of the air in my lungs whooshed out. My skates flew up and out from under me. For a moment that seemed like an hour, I was floating in the air. Then I slammed into the boards. The crash rattled every bone in my body. I felt like a cup of dice in a Yahtzee game. The first hit centered on my chest, but when I hit those boards, there was no center. The collision reverberated from my heels to my hands to my head. Even my teeth hurt.

I crumpled to the ice. For some reason, the ice was spinning. My vision narrowed suddenly, as if two black walls were closing in on me. It seemed as if the two sides touched just briefly, then pulled back and faded.

I didn't hear a whistle, but all of the sudden, Coach Andy's concerned face was hovering above me. "Sam? I said, can you hear me?"

"Ayuh," I mumbled.

He held up about eleven fingers and asked me how many I saw.

"Four," I guessed.

The concern on his face didn't change, but he masked it with a smile. "All right. You're going to be fine. Just lay here for a second, and then we'll get you off the ice. Okay?"

"Okay," I said.

I laid there for a few seconds, then I asked, "Coach?"

"What?"

"Did I score?"

8

My head felt like it was going to explode. The slightest movement shot pain all around my noggin. I sat in the furthest corner doctor's office waiting room with my eyes closed, trying to hide from all the sound. A television was blaring. In the middle of the room, a baby kept crying. Every so often, a nurse came out of the back and shouted names.

I felt like I was going to puke.

When I opened my eyes, a kid, probably about three or four years old, stood in front of me. He grinned and thrust his plastic toy toward me. "Play fire truck?"

Even with my head throbbing, I could see that the toy he held was several Legos stuck together. They were the big kind that parents buy when kids are too young for the real thing.

The kid kept staring at me, grinning. A stream of clear snot trickled out his nose, but he sniffed it back up.

"Fire truck?" he asked me again.

I shook my head to say no. That was a mistake. For starters, the motion hurt like crazy. I closed my eyes again and brought my hands to my head. Then the kid started to cry right there in front of me. The whining, hitching sound echoed around in my head like a bowling ball in a dryer.

"Eldred, come here!" A woman's voice bellowed over the top of the kid's crying. That was like someone threw five hundred marbles into that dryer to go along with the bowling ball. "Leave that poor boy alone."

"No!" Eldred said obstinately.

Bowling ball. *Klunk-ku-klunk!*

"Young man, you get your rear end over here now!" His mother snapped.

Marbles. *Ka-kling-ka-klack-slam!*

I opened my eyes just in time to see a defeated Eldred hang his head and drag his feet toward his mother. He didn't look too happy at the idea, either. I guess I wouldn't be too happy either, if my Mom had named me Eldred.

The TV kept blaring, people kept coughing, Eldred kept misbehaving while his mother kept correcting him and the nurse kept yelling. I closed my eyes and thought about the reason I was there.

Coach Andy took me off the ice after the hit. I felt a little shaky while I changed into my clothes, but he said that was normal. When the rest of the team came in, Coach Valka congratulated us on our first win of the season. He awarded me the game puck for "potting a couple of goals and giving the body as good as he got."

I wasn't so sure, but I smiled weakly and put the puck in my bag.

Coach Andy had a talk with my parents. Afterward, they were both jittery. Mom especially. She fawned all over me while Dad carried my bag and my sticks out of the rink. He hadn't done that since I was five and I was too little to carry the gear all by myself.

I spent that afternoon on the couch, watching TV and drinking lots of water. Mom said it was water or chamomile tea. I thought chamomile tea tasted like strained weeds, so I voted for water. Mom brought tea, anyway. After a while, I started feeling a little nauseous. My head started to hurt so bad that I switched off the TV. Mom was in the room in an instant, asking if I was all right. I told her how I felt. It seemed like we were at the doctor's office about ten seconds later.

"Eldred, stop that! Let that boy be. Can't you see he's sick?"

"Fire truck?" I heard Eldred ask someone.

I swallowed, wishing I had some earplugs.

It was Nate that hit me. That's what Jill told me in the locker room after the game. Coach Andy said he didn't know which player it was. Coach Valka said it was a clean hit, but I didn't know how it could be clean if I never saw it coming.

Over and over again, I tried to figure out how it happened.

I remembered reaching for the puck, but bobbling it because of the grooves in the ice. That slowed me down. The knot in my calf probably slowed me down some, too, though that injury felt like a stubbed toe in comparison to the way my head felt now.

I could remember getting control of the puck and turning...

"Honey?" My Mom's voice blared at me and I jumped. Forget bowling balls and marbles. That was like slamming the dryer door six times.

"Yeah?" I whispered.

"Oh, sorry," she said, lowering her voice. "I'm finished talking to the doctor. Are you ready to go?"

"Yeah."

We left the doctor's office, leaving behind one final, plaintive request from Eldred.

"Fire truck?"

We didn't speak on the ride home. I felt a little weird, almost as if I were in a movie, watching everything happen to me. The businesses and homes flitted by the window as I watched from that strange zone.

Once we were home and through the front door, Mom told me the doctor said it was best that

I keep calm and quiet. She gave me some aspirin and smiled through her worried expression.

"Mom?"

"Yes, honey?"

"What's wrong with me?"

Some of her smile went away and some more worry replaced it. "The doctor said you have a mild concussion."

I blinked. "A concussion?"

"Yes," she said. "He said that it was the reaction to your brain getting jarred when that boy hit you."

"And this is a *mild* one?" If this was a mild version, I made up my mind right then to avoid the severe version. Or even the medium one.

"That's what he said." Her face grew more concerned. "Why? Do you feel worse than you told him? Do you have new symptoms?"

"No," I said immediately.

Her expression softened slightly. "All right. Well, he said you need to rest today and tomorrow. After that, it depends on how you feel. If your symptoms don't go away, we'll need to go back to see him again."

"I have practice tomorrow."

She shook her head firmly. "No, you don't. No hockey until this is cleared up. Doctor's orders."

I frowned. Doctor's orders weren't such a big thing, but I could tell from the sound of her voice that these were also Mom's orders, and those carried considerable weight.

"Go rest," she said. "I'll bring you some chamomile tea."

Yuck, I thought, but I didn't even have the strength to argue.

9

The next two days were the strangest and most boring days of my life. Watching TV or playing video games made me feel sick or made my head hurt. So did reading. Music was too loud. Mom wouldn't let Jill come over, either. So there were long stretches of boredom. I learned more about every swirling pattern on the ceiling of my bedroom than I ever thought possible.

I tried to sleep, but it didn't always happen.

At other times, I experienced that strange, sort of floating sensation. I felt like I was outside myself, watching me. Mom told me the doctor called it a "dissociative" feeling and that it was normal for someone who suffered a concussion.

Mostly I sat on my bed. Or in the chair at my desk. Sometimes I mixed it up and lay on my bed. Other times, when I was feeling disassociated, I watched myself sit on the bed. Or the chair. Or lay on the bed.

It sucked worse than summer.

Over and over again, I relived the bone-crushing hit from Nate. I remembered the piercing pain in my chest that came first. That's how I figured out he must have hit me from the front, which I guess made it a clean check. Still, the way it rattled my teeth, squeezed all the air out of me and sent me flying into the boards didn't seem too clean to me.

Colliding with the boards had been the worst part. I woke up twice that first night from dreams of being blasted into the boards again. In the second dream, I left a big dent in them.

I didn't tell Mom about the dreams. I didn't tell Dad, either. I didn't want them to worry.

On the second day, I felt a little better. I got on the computer for a little while and googled 'hockey concussions.' I read about player after player who were forced into early retirement from the NHL because of 'post-concussion syndrome.' Alex Ridley. Eric Lindros. Keith Primeau. All big guys.

I didn't like that idea one bit.

There was even an article about one of my favorite Spokane Chiefs players of all time, Alex Ridley. He'd worn number ten and scored a goal in the very first game I can remember going to when I was about five. He was Jill's favorite player, too. I knew he went on to play in the pros, but I sort of lost track of him after he left Spokane.

According to the article, Alex Ridley played a year of minor league hockey in the AHL before being called up to the NHL. He played a total of 62 games over two different seasons for the Philadelphia Flyers before retiring due to post-concussion syndrome.

Alex Ridley. I met him once at the Spokane Arena. He had some kind of arm or shoulder injury, because he was wearing a sling under the suit jacket he had on. He and a couple of other players were walking around the concourse in between periods when my dad pointed them out.

"Know who that is?" Dad asked me.

I didn't recognize him off the ice and not in uniform, but I knew by the suits they all three wore that they were Chiefs players.

"That's your favorite," Dad told me. "That's Ridder."

We approached the three of them and said hello. They all said hello. Pretty soon, a few other kids clustered around. Someone came up with a sharpie pen and suddenly all three players were signing jerseys and programs. I got my "Alex Ridley #10" signature right in the middle of my chest for all to see. Jill was jealous that she missed out.

Wow. Alex Ridley quit hockey because of a concussion.

I heard someone coming, so I clicked over to the Nickelodeon page. It was Dad. He had a sandwich and some chamomile tea.

"How're you feeling, champ?"

"Better," I said, closing down the Internet. "In fact, I think I'm good enough to stop drinking chamomile tea."

Dad smiled. "Really?"

I nodded. Carefully.

Dad set the plate on my desk. "Does your head still hurt?"

"A little," I admitted.

"Feeling nauseous?"

"Not really."

"How about that spacey feeling? Is that gone?"

"Mostly."

"Well, then," he said, setting the tea cup next to the sandwich, "it sounds like your Mom's magic tea is working."

I bit back a groan. More strained weeds.

Dad stood there for a minute like he wanted to say something. Then he reached out, gave my shoulder a gentle squeeze and left the room.

10

By the third day, all my symptoms were gone. Mom asked me about a million times, but every time she did, I felt fine. No headache. No nausea. No spacey feeling. I said I was ready to go back to school and to play hockey. She called the doctor's office to be sure, then reluctantly agreed.

At school, I met Jill near the teeter-totters. That was our spot. No one hardly played on them, anyway.

I told her what the doctor said and how my concussion felt. When I described the spacey feeling, her eyes got big.

"Wow. That's weird."

"It felt weird, that's for sure."

"But you're okay to play hockey again?"

I nodded.

Jill glanced around to see if we were alone. Then she lowered her voice. "Aren't you scared?" she asked. "I mean, that it might happen again?"

I blinked at her. I'd spent so much time thinking about what had happened that it never occurred to me that it could happen again. "No," I said, even though a tremor of icy fear fluttered in my stomach.

"Not at all?"

"No," I repeated, a little stronger this time. Images of Nate slamming me into the boards over and over flashed through my mind.

She shook her head. "Wow. I think I would be."

"Maybe that's the difference between girls and boys," I said, without thinking.

Jill's eyes widened in surprise. Then a hurt expression flickered across her face. Both gave way quickly to narrowing eyes and an angry stare. "Maybe the difference is that boys are stupid jerks," she said. Then she turned and stomped away. Her long braid bounced and swayed with each angry step.

I sighed.

Great. Not only did I have to worry about getting creamed on the ice again, but my best friend was mad at me, too.

After about ten steps, Jill stopped. She paused for a few moments, then turned and stalked back toward me. When she reached the teeter-totters, she looked me in the eye. "If you say you're sorry now, I'll believe you only said that other thing because you just had your brains scrambled. Otherwise –"

"I'm sorry," I said immediately, and I meant it.

Her expression softened. "Okay." Then she smiled. "Wanna teeter-totter?"

After school, I was alone at the house for about an hour. I had a snack and read some more about concussions on the Internet. Nothing that I found out made me feel any better. One article said that once you've had one concussion, it made you more susceptible to future ones. It also said that each time you had a concussion, the symptoms could be worse and could last longer.

I sat at my desk and stared at the computer.

This was worse than I thought. It was like I had some kind of a debilitating disease or something. How was I supposed to keep my parents from getting a divorce now?

11

The Rockets lost their second game. I missed it because of my concussion. Jill told me about it at school the next day.

"How bad was it?" I asked.

She grimaced. "3-1."

"That doesn't sound so bad."

Jill tilted her head. "Well..."

I looked at her closer. "Are you saying it wasn't that close?"

She shook her head. "We were kinda lucky that they only scored three. They had a lot of shots."

"So brilliant goaltending saved the day?" I asked her, sort of teasing, but sort of not.

She shrugged. "I had a really good game. Dad said I was 'in the zone.'"

I smiled at her. In spite of everything that was going on, I was glad to see her getting comfortable as a goalie. "It fits you," I told her.

"What?"

"Being a goalie. It fits you."

She smiled. "Thanks. I like it. It's fun." She paused. "We could have used you, though. Besides you and maybe Carson, no one on our team is very good at scoring goals."

"Coach says it's a team sport," I said.

"Yup," Jill said, "but the problem is that no one else on our team is very good at scoring goals."

"Well," I said, "I'm coming back to practice tomorrow."

"Good," Jill said. "It's not the same without you there." She gave me a playful slug on the shoulder. It made my stomach feel a little funny when she did that.

I gave her one back and smiled.

The next day at practice, I had mixed emotions. It felt good to put on my skates and equipment. The hockey stick rested comfortably in my hands. The first few laps around the rink with the cold air blowing in my face actually made me smile.

Then we started drills.

Every time someone came near me when I had the puck, I winced, expecting to get blasted. My stomach was a mess, like it was filled with battery acid or something. The slightest bump or nudge from another player made me tense up. Barely half way through the practice, I was already exhausted.

Coach Andy took me aside during the water break. He grinned at me. "It's a little tough getting back into the swing of things, huh?"

I nodded. "A little."

He patted me on the shoulder. "You have to try to relax. Just play the game the way you always have and you'll be fine."

"Okay," I said. I thought about what I read on the Internet about concussions. "Coach?" I asked.

"Yes?"

"Do you know much about concussions?"

He nodded. "Sure. What did you want to know?"

I swallowed. "It's just...well, I read on the Internet about how if you get one, it's easier to get a second one."

He nodded.

"And that the second one can be worse and last longer," I continued.

He nodded again.

"And I read about guys like Alex Ridley and Eric Lindros and Keith Primeau all having to retire from the NHL."

"I read that, too," Coach Andy said. He gave me a warm smile. "Sam, those players had severe concussions, many times worse than what I understood yours to be. Regular people get mild concussions all the time with no long-lasting effects. It's not a good thing, but it is minor in comparison." He patted my shoulder. "You should be fine. But if you want to take a couple of weeks off, I don't see anything wrong with that."

A couple of *weeks*? My parents might be completely divorced by then.

I shook my head. "No, thanks. I was just wondering, is all."

"Okay," Coach Andy said. He gave me an inquisitive look, then tapped me on the helmet. "Go get some water."

Dinner time had changed. It was never something that excited me very much before. In fact, it was usually something that got in the way of whatever I was trying to do. Sometimes it was watching a TV show or playing a video game. Sometimes Jill was over and dinner time meant that she had to go home. Whatever the case, dinner time wasn't exactly a celebration.

Before, Mom and Dad talked about work. They asked me about school. One of them, usually Dad, asked me if I'd done my homework yet. Sometimes we talked about hockey. If it was later in the week, we'd plan things for the weekend.

Things were different now. It was like there was an invisible, heavy fog surrounding the table. Mom and Dad spoke very little. The sound of forks and knives against our plates clicked and clacked loudly in the room.

"First practice back today?" Dad finally broke the silence.

"Yeah," I answered.

"How'd it go?"

"Fine, I guess." I shrugged. "It was just a practice."

Dad nodded and made grunting sound. He took a bite of salad and crunched noisily.

"Actually," Mom said, "I talked with Coach Andy after practice today while you were changing." She glanced over at me. "He said you had a little trepidation about playing."

I swallowed. I didn't know what 'trepidation' meant, but I was guessing it meant something like 'scared.'

"Not surprising that he'd be a little tentative," Dad said before I could answer. "Taking a big hit like that can rattle a person."

Mom didn't reply right away. She just looked at me. I squirmed in my seat. Finally, I remembered Coach Andy's words. "It's no big deal," I said. "I just need to relax and play the game my way."

"Right," Dad said, cutting into his meat.

"I don't know," Mom said. "I wonder if it might not be a bad idea for Sam to take a break from playing. Just to be safe."

I opened my mouth to answer, but Dad beat me to it.

"Oh, I don't think so," he said, his voice a little sharper than usual. "The best thing for him to do is to get right back in the saddle again."

Mom put her fork down. "I'm not talking about psychological issues here, Roger. That's a completely different discussion and one I'm not convinced you're right about."

"Karen—" Dad said, but she cut him off.

"I'm talking about his physical health." She pointed at me. "He just suffered a major trauma to the head –"

"He had a mild concussion," Dad interrupted. "It happens to people all over the world every day of the week."

"I'm not interested in who else it has happened to. What I'm interested in is the fact that it happened to our son. And I don't think he's quite ready to be playing hockey yet."

"The doctor said he was fine," Dad said.

"That's his opinion."

"His *professional* opinion," Dad emphasized. "Sam's fine."

I watched in amazement, my gaze going back and forth between the two of them.

"What if he isn't healed up yet?" Mom asked.

"The doctor said he is. He says he is. I'll bet Coach Andy said he is, too."

Mom shook her head. "He said no such thing. We talked more about Sam's mental state, anyway."

"Well, then I'm confused," Dad said. "First you said you're concerned about his physical health and now it's his mental state you're worried about."

"It's both, Roger. The truth is, I'm surprised that you're not worried, too."

Dad shrugged. "Injuries are a part of sports, Karen. They happen. You heal up and get right back out there. That's hockey. That's life."

"Well, if he's going to keep getting hurt like this, maybe he should quit playing hockey altogether," Mom snapped.

"He's not quitting," Dad snapped back.

The two of them stared at each other across the table in cold silence. I swallowed heavily. My head was spinning. My stomach hurt. I thought for a minute that maybe I was having a concussion relapse or something.

Both of my parents seemed to notice me again at the same time. As soon as that happened, they exchanged a sheepish look. Dad cleared his throat. Mom picked up her fork again.

"We'll talk about this later," she said quietly.

Dad nodded in agreement.

Like I said, dinner time wasn't the same any more.

12

The Sharks were the best team in the league last year. Coach Valka said that they were even better this year.

"It's going to take a team effort to beat these guys," he told us in the locker room. "No one-man shows out there."

He pointed at Jill. "Your goaltender can not win the game all by herself. You defensemen have got to clear the puck out of the zone every chance you get. But do it with control. Hit the winger or the center with a pass. And I want to see you clear out that crease. If there's a man standing near your goalie, you push him out of the way. If the puck is nearby, you dump him on his backside. Clear?"

"Yes, Coach!"

Coach Valka continued. "Forwards, make sure you come back defensively. And when you get into the offensive zone, shoot the puck at the net.

Anyone remember what Wayne Gretzky said about shooting?"

No one answered.

Coach Valka glanced to his assistant. "Andy?"

Coach Andy smiled. "Well, he said a lot of things, but probably the most famous is this – you miss one hundred percent of the shots you don't take."

We sat quietly for a moment, thinking about what that meant. It took a moment to realize it wasn't a math problem or something.

"What's that mean?" Coach Valka asked the group.

No one raised a hand. After a moment, Coach Valka answered his own question. "It means that if you don't shoot, you can't score. So put the puck on net. Got it?"

"Yes, Coach!"

I looked down at my skates, thinking about what Wayne Gretzky had said. Coach Valka was right, I knew, but somehow I felt like there was more to it than that. I didn't have time to think about it, though, because Coach Valka had us up and out the door.

As I walked down the corridor and toward the ice rink, butterflies flip-flopped in my stomach. Not the good kind, which are expectant, warm and exciting. These were the heavy, cold kind that felt more like icy razor blades flapping than butterfly wings.

I took a deep breath and let it out.

It didn't help.

When we hit the ice, I skated hard on my first two laps around our end of the rink. I wanted to show everyone on the team that I could bounce back. I wanted the Coach to know I was pumped up for the game, even if cold dread sat in my stomach like a pile of steel marbles.

Most of all, I wanted my parents to see my zipping around the ice so they'd be proud of me. Maybe it wasn't too late for my plan to keep them together to work out. I hadn't heard them fighting, like Kayla's parents did. Maybe things weren't set in stone yet.

All I had to do is have a great game.

Coach Valka started Carson's line, so I sat on the bench, squeezing my stick nervously and watching the play. It seemed like it took forever for Coach Valka to call for a line change, but then suddenly I was on the ice.

I skated toward their center, who was carrying the puck. He was a big kid, maybe even bigger than Nate. He handled the puck clumsily, telegraphing the pass he was about to make. I swooped to my right in an arc. When he made a lazy pass to his left winger, I dropped to a knee and stretched my stick out along the ice. The puck clacked into my stick just above the blade. I rose to my feet, turned my skate blade sideways and gave the puck a gentle kick forward to my stick.

I heard the center yell in surprise, then anger, but I was past him before he could even change direction. One of their defenseman was playing high, so he was out of position to defend against my rush up ice. That left one defenseman to beat.

He skated backwards confidently, his stick out in front of him. I faked to my right, then chipped the puck right between his legs and went left. Instead of sticking with me, he tried to stop the puck by squeezing his legs together. He wasn't quick enough. The puck landed behind him and skittered down the ice.

I flew past the defenseman as he turned around and tried to catch up. When I reach the puck, I nudged it forward. Then I glanced over my shoulder. He was bearing down on me, but I had room to make the shot. I skated two more strides, cradled the puck and ripped it.

The goalie lunged at the puck with his glove, but missed.

I started to raise my arms in celebration.

Tink!

The puck struck the crossbar and bounced back. No goal.

Before I had time to think, the rebound landed on my stick. A chance to fire it again. No time to aim, just shovel it toward the goal and hope for the best –

The hit came from the side. The defenseman I managed to get around caught up to me. With the puck on my stick, I was fair game. He crunched into me, knocking the air out of my chest. Jarring pain reverberated through my upper body. The force of the blow sent me sprawling on the ice. That didn't hurt as bad as the boards, but if still felt like the wind got knocked out of me a second time.

I lay on the ice, unmoving. The hardest thing about losing your wind is the way it messes with your mind. I knew that in a few more seconds, I'd get my breath back. But I felt panic rising from my stomach into my chest as I struggled to breathe. It was probably a good thing I didn't have any air in my lungs, because I would have screamed.

A few moments later, a whistle blew. I knew it was for me. Any time there was an injured player, the ref stopped the game. The coach would come onto the ice and check things out. If necessary, so would a doctor. In our case, with Coach Andy, it could be the same guy.

I willed myself to breathe.

Nothing happened.

I willed myself to get up.

I couldn't move.

Another shot of panic went through me. What if it wasn't a concussion this time? What if I was paralyzed or something?

I had an image of me in a wheelchair flash through my mind. On the tail end of that came a crazy thought; my parents wouldn't get divorced if I was disabled, would they?

I managed to wiggle my feet, flopping the skates from side to side, dispelling that theory. A moment later, I saw a shadow loom over me. Coach Andy knelt down.

"You okay, Sam?"

The beginnings of a breath started to seep back into my lungs, but it wasn't enough to talk yet. Instead, I just nodded.

"Where do you hurt?" he asked.

I reached up and tapped my chest with my gloved hand.

Coach Andy nodded. "Feel like something broke?"

I shook my head.

"Got your wind knocked out?"

I nodded. As I did, the first halting breath of air came back into me. So I said, "I'm okay, Coach." It came out as more of a wheeze but at least I made a sound.

Coach Andy smiled. "Okay. You want to get up?"

"Yeah," I said with my second good breath.

I sat up and Coach Andy helped me to my skates. A smattering of light applause from the spectators and some stick-tapping on the ice from the players accompanied the move. I skated slowly toward the bench and took a seat.

Coach Valka put his hand on my shoulder. "Way to read the pass, Parker."

"Thanks, Coach."

"And good shot."

"Thanks, Coach," I said, but I thought, *It didn't go in, though.*

I kept taking deep breaths on the bench. After a minute or so, my breathing felt normal again. But my entire upper body felt like one big bruise. That same unsettling fear I had before the game rested in my stomach. All I could think was how I was going to keep getting hit like that through the whole game. And the game after that. And the one after that. And one of those hits, maybe the next one, was going to be a like the Nate Bridger hit.

Or worse.

"First line," Coach Valka called. "Get out there!"

We scrambled through a line change. One of our defensemen had the puck. As soon as he made it across the red line at center ice, he shot the puck into the near corner of the offensive zone. I turned on the jets and headed for the puck. Out of the corner of my eye, I saw their defenseman doing the same. It was going to be a close race, but I knew I was faster than him.

As we got closer to the puck, he changed his skating angle slightly. Instead of racing toward the puck, he was focused on me. It felt like he had target lock on the center of my chest. I glanced at the puck, lying in the corner along the boards. Was I fast enough to beat him to it clean and skate away with it? Or was he going to staple me to the boards as soon as we both got to the puck?

I thought I could hear his breath coming. It reminded me of a bull, charging toward one of those guys with the red cape.

Without thinking, I pulled up slightly and looked directly at the defensemen. He ignored me and skated hard. He covered the remaining distance to the puck in a split second, scooped it up and skated behind his own net. I stood near the corner and watched, relieved.

I heard the Coach yelling my name, but I couldn't make out the words. His barking voice broke me out of my reverie, though, and I started up ice. The defenseman made a nice pass to his center, who had no one on him because that's where I was supposed to be. I lowered my head and skated hard to catch up.

They were too far ahead, though.

The center and both of his wingers skated into our zone against just our two defensemen. It was a three-on-two situation and that meant that one of their guys was always going to be open.

This time it was the left winger, who darted into the slot while the center skated wide. He saw the winger and passed it directly to him. The winger caught the pass. I watched helplessly from center ice. Before Jill could slide across to make a play, the winger flicked the puck into the upper part of the net.

Goal.

Celebration and hoopla broke out on the Sharks bench and from their fans. I hung my head immediately, knowing that goal was my fault.

Back on the bench, Coach Valka knew it, too.

"You're the center because you're the fastest skater, Parker!" he bellowed at me. "You've got to get to the puck first. And if you can't do that, then you better get back defensively. Not stand there like a spectator." He jabbed a finger at me. "You want to watch the game, go sit in the stands. Got me?"

"Yes, Coach," I mumbled.

On the next shift, I won the face-off in our own zone. The 'D' sent a pass right back to me and we started up ice. Both of my wingers were covered, but I could see that the left wing was faster than his opponent. If I hung onto the puck for a few seconds, he should be open for a pass.

To my right, the hulking frame of the Sharks center barreled toward me. A simple equation kept bouncing through my head. I had the puck. He was going to hit me. I had the puck. He was going to hit me. I had the puck. He was going to —

I couldn't stand it. Panic shot through my stomach. It seemed to continue right out to my arms. Without thinking, I passed blindly up the boards to no one.

Their defenseman easily recovered the puck amidst groans from my own bench.

Back on the bench, Coach Valka let me have it. "Make good passes!" he barked. "It makes no sense to give away the puck!"

I tried, but every shift was the same. I lost all of the close races to the puck, no matter where it was on the ice. I didn't want to get creamed. When I had the puck, I dished it off as soon as I could. I knew that if I didn't have the puck, I couldn't be hit.

After a while, Coach Valka stopped correcting me between shifts. Instead, I sat on the bench, looking down between my skates.

Come on, I thought. *Get in the game.*

Then I'd go out for another shift and it would be the same. I pulled up short on a race to the puck so that the other guy couldn't check me. Or I made a quick pass to avoid handling the puck. Then it was back to the bench, where I looked down at my skates and yelled at myself inside my head.

It used to be that I wanted to have the puck every chance I could. That black disc on my stick blade sent a thrill through me. Now, it was like it came with a giant bulls-eye attached to it. I got rid of it as soon as I could. I was relieved when the other team had possession so that all I had to do was play defensively instead of carrying the puck.

When the horn sounded at the end of the game, I looked up at the scoreboard. It read, Sharks – 1, Rockets – 0.

In the locker room after the game, Jill didn't sit by me. Instead, she sat in the open space near the door. We all listened to the Coach briefly run over what we did well and what we did poorly. Although he didn't stare at me while he spoke, everything he said on the poor side applied directly to me.

"When there's a fifty-fifty puck, we need to win those races," he said.

"We need to hold onto the puck a little longer and make good passes," he said.

I kept staring at my skates. I could feel every eye in the locker room on me as Coach Valka spoke.

"Don't be shy about body checking their players when they have the puck and we're on defense," he said.

"We can't win if we don't score goals," he said.

I glanced up at Jill. She was staring at me with an expression that was hard to read. I couldn't tell if it was anger or concern or some combination of both.

I looked away.

After he was finished, Coach Valka left the room. Jill followed, headed to the girl's locker room. No one said anything to me. I changed in silence as quickly as I could. Then I picked up my bag and headed for the door. It seemed like it took forever to find my sticks in the jumbled stack near the door. I felt every eye boring into the back of my head. Finally, I found my sticks and left the locker room.

Coach Andy sat in a bleacher seat nearby, reading a book. When he saw me, he waved me over. "Coach Valka wants to see you," he told me.

Uh-oh.

I swallowed and nodded. Dread filled my stomach. Getting called into the coach's office was way worse than getting sent to the principal's office at school. Like about a billion times worse.

The door to Coach Valka's office was closed. I set my bag down and put my sticks on top of it. Then I knocked lightly on the door.

"Come!"

I opened the door but didn't step in. The office was the size of a large closet. Coach Valka's desk took up almost the entire room. Two small plastic chairs sat against the wall in front of his desk. A picture of Mark Messier hung on the wall. Shelves of neatly stacked and labeled binders lined the rest of the walls. Coach Valka sat behind the desk, pencil in hand, writing on a yellow notepad.

"Sit down, Parker," he said without looking up.

I moved toward the plastic chair.

"Close the door first," he said, still not looking at me.

I gulped silently. The only thing worse than getting called to the coach's office was having a talk with the coach with the door closed.

I had to press my back to the wall to make room for the door to get past me. The resounding metal click of the latch and the rumbling thud of the wooden door echoed, filling the office with a foreboding sound. I sat down and waited.

After a few moments, Coach Valka put down his pencil and looked up at me. "What does a coach do, Parker?" he asked me. His voice has an edge to it, even though the volume was normal.

I tried to understand his question. He stared at me, waiting. Finally, I answered, "A coach...coaches."

What a lame answer, I thought. But I couldn't come up with anything better with him staring at me like that.

"A coach coaches," Coach Valka repeated. Then he nodded. "That's right. A coach *teaches* the player the game. He *directs* the player. He *corrects* the player. And what does the player do?"

I knew the answer, but I couldn't say it.

I didn't have to, because Coach Valka answered for me. "The player *listens*. In fact, that's one our team's cardinal rules, isn't it?"

I nodded.

Coach Valka held up a finger and counted them off. "Come to practice. Skate Hard. Listen to the coaches. Remember?"

I nodded again.

He pointed at me. "And you're not listening, Parker."

I didn't say anything. I didn't know how to explain to him that I *was* listening. I just couldn't make my body do what he was telling me.

"I understand that you took a big check a couple of games ago," he went on. "And that can rattle a player sometimes. But I've got an entire team to think about. That team is counting on me. And they're counting on you."

He was right and I knew it.

"I'm sorry, Coach," I said glumly.

Coach Valka shook his head. "Sorry was yesterday's news. Today is something different."

What does *that* mean?

Before I had a chance to try to figure it out, Coach Valka answered that question for me, too. "I'm benching you," he said.

I gaped at him. "Bu—bu—benching me?"

He nodded. "Effective immediately. You can come to practices and work hard, but until I'm convinced you can listen, you don't dress for any games."

"But Coach—"

He picked up his pencil and looked back down at his notepad. "That's all, Parker."

I sat in stunned silence.

Benched?

I shook my head. This couldn't be happening to me. First my parents are getting a divorce. Then Nate Bridger lays me out and gives me a concussion. And now *this*? The coach is *benching* me?

"That's not fair," I whispered.

Coach Valka stopped writing and looked up. He didn't say a word. He only looked at me with those hard eyes of his. His stare usually reminded me of what an ant must feel like when some kid fries it with a magnifying glass. But then I felt something different in my stomach. Something other than the cold electricity of fear. I felt a warm spark of anger, like someone struck a match in there.

"That's not fair," I said, a little louder.

I didn't necessarily *like* feeling angry, but at the moment, it felt a whole lot better than being afraid.

Coach Valka's expression didn't change. "It's not about fair, Parker," he said. "It's about what is."

The warm feeling in my stomach flared up to a bonifire. I spoke without thinking.

"Well, maybe I'll just quit this stupid team!" I snapped.

Surprise registered on Coach Valka's face.

Before he could answer, I stood and left the office, slamming the door behind me.

13

Dinner time that night was tense and quiet. Dad scowled at the news of my benching, but I could have sworn I saw a flash of relief in my Mom's expression. I didn't tell them about the way the conversation with Coach Valka ended.

We ate our food. There were a few stilted, polite exchanges.

When I couldn't stand it anymore, I asked to be excused. In my room, I sat on the edge of my bed. I felt like crying, but didn't want to give in to it. The feeling hung in my chest, nibbling at me. I tried to sort out my feelings, but there were too many different ones. They flew at me from different directions. None of them stayed long enough to figure out before getting bumped aside by a different one.

The coach benched me, but after what I said to him, he might kick me off the team. That meant no more hockey.

But I loved hockey.

But it also meant no more getting hit.

No more being afraid.

On the other hand, it meant not playing with Jill.

And what about my plan? How could I keep my parents together if I couldn't play?

My parents probably weren't very proud of me right now. In fact, they were probably ashamed. And I'm sure Coach Valka was mad at me. So were all my teammates. I'm sure Jill was, too.

I let out a long, wavering sigh. Somehow, a tear had snuck out and I wiped it from my cheek.

To take my mind off of everything, I fired up my videogame player. Flying around in a space ship and blasting robots for an hour was much better than thinking about all of this.

I cleared four levels on the hard setting before I needed to use the bathroom. As I walked down the hall, I heard my parents talking in the living room. I paused at the top of the stairs, listening. It was wrong and I knew it, but I couldn't stop myself. Especially when I realized they were talking about me.

"You have to expect some difficulty adjusting," Dad said. "Anger is a part of that."

"I'm just worried," Mom said. "He's never been a particularly angry kid."

"Everyone has a temper. This is a big event for him. It can be a lot to handle for an eleven year old."

"I understand that," Mom replied. "He *is* only eleven. It's easy for things to pile up for him."

"Still, I don't think this hockey situation has anything to do with the divorce," Dad said. "I think they are two separate things. And so we should treat them that way."

"I don't know if they're separate or not," said Mom.

"Are you saying that because you think it or because you want to argue about it?"

"I don't want to argue about anything, Roger."

"That's part of the problem."

"No," Mom said, "the problem is that you want to argue about *everything*."

"No," Dad said, "the problem is that you can't be wrong about *anything*."

There was a short silence. Mom broke it first. "Let's just focus on our son, okay?"

"Fine."

"Good."

There was another silence. Then Mom said, "Now that there's all this body checking going on, I think hockey is just too dangerous. I think we should take him out for his own good."

"So he should just quit?"

"Yes. Before he gets really hurt."

I stood stock-still, my heart racing. Thoughts jumbled around inside my head and emotions swirled in my chest.

I wanted to shout "NO!" at Mom. I love hockey. I can't quit.

And yet, at the same time, relief washed over me. I could quit. Mom said it was okay. I wouldn't have to get hit again.

"No," Dad said forcefully. "That's exactly the wrong thing to do. If he quits now, all he's learning is that when life gets tough, that's how you handle things."

"Sometimes it's the best solution to a problem," Mom said quietly. "Look at us."

"That's different," Dad said.

"Not so much."

"Anyway," Dad said, "we can understand the nuances of things like this. Sam is still impressionable."

"I think he's more mature than you give him credit for."

"Mature or not, he's eleven."

"What else did his coach say when you called him?" Mom asked.

My ears pricked up even further. They talked to Coach Valka?

"Andy said that he was welcome back on the team," Dad said.

I brightened at the sound of that.

"What about his conversation with the coach?" Mom asked.

"Andy only said that he and Steve think that Sam needs a little more time to recover from the emotional impact of the concussion."

"Which is what I said a few days ago," Mom said.

"Which is what you said a few days go," Dad repeated. "Yes. So what?"

"I'm just saying that you should trust me a little more when it comes to these things. When we're living apart, it's going to be even more important."

Living apart?

Those two words rang in my ears. They were still planning on getting a divorce. I'd done nothing to change either of their minds.

"Let's deal with what's in front of us first, shall we?" Dad said.

"Fine."

"Good."

There was another silence. I thought that it was quiet enough for them to hear my breathing at the top of the stairs. Then they resumed talking.

"Let's give him a few days and see how things are," Mom suggested.

"I'm all right with giving him a few days, but he needs to get back on the ice," Dad said. "That's life, Karen."

"Yes, you said that before."

"I mean it."

Mom sighed. "I think we should leave it up to him. Don't you?"

Dad was quiet for a long while. I stood as still as possible. Anyone walking by would have thought I was a Sam statue at the top of the stairs.

Finally, Dad spoke. "All right. We'll let him choose. Your way or mine."

"Fine," Mom said.

"Good," Dad replied.

I forgot about going to the bathroom. Instead, I crept back to my room. I sat on the edge of my bed. That nagging feeling that I wanted to cry quit nibbling at me. Instead, it gobbled me up.

14

I didn't sleep very well that night. At breakfast, I ate part of a pop tart before I caught the bus. All around me, kids were laughing and screaming. I looked around and wondered how many of them had parents who were divorced. Probably none. That's probably why they thought a stupid bus ride to school was so much fun.

The first two class periods dragged by. After that, we got a fifteen minute recess. I hurried straight out to the teeter-totters. I needed to talk to Jill. She wasn't there.

I stood on top of the center of the teeter-totter and scanned the playground for her. I looked for her signature braid, but it was nowhere to be found.

After what seemed like forever, she exited the building and sauntered over.

"Where have you been?" I snapped.

Her eyes narrowed slightly.

"Recess is just about over," I said, frustrated.

She frowned. "I had to take a quiz in Mrs. Plumb's class," she said in a low voice.

"Fine," I said, waving away her explanation. "Did you hear what happened yesterday?"

"You mean how you decided to let the Sharks beat us?"

I gawked at her. "What?"

"I was there, Sam. I saw the whole thing."

"But..." I didn't know what to say. I knew Coach Valka wouldn't understand. I knew my parents couldn't understand. But I figured Jill would always understand.

"You said you weren't afraid," Jill said. "But you are. At least admit it."

"You don't understand," I said.

"I do, too," Jill said. "You're afraid but you won't admit it."

"I'm not afraid."

Jill paused, chewing on the inside of her lip. "I suppose it's okay to be scared," she said. "Like I said before, I think I would be."

She looked at me, as if to challenge me to repeat my stupid remark about boys and girls. I played it smart and changed the subject. "I meant *after* the game. Did you hear?"

Jill squinted inquisitively. "After? No. What happened?"

I took a deep breath. "Coach Valka called me to his office."

Her eyes widened. "Really?"

I was glad to have the chance to talk to someone about it, and who better than my best friend? But just then, the bell rang. I gave her an exasperated look. She shrugged. "See ya at lunch?"

I sighed. "See ya."

The next two class periods lasted about a century a piece. By the time we let out for lunch, I was crawling out of my skin.

This time, Jill was waiting for me at the teeter-totter, crunching on an apple.

I told her about my meeting with the coach. Her eyes grew big, but she didn't interrupt. Then I told her about my parents' conversation that I overheard. She nodded sympathetically. "Just like Kayla's parents."

I shook my head. "That's not the point," I said.

"What is?"

"Don't you see?" I told her. "They're making me choose."

Jill gave me a confused look. "Well, that's an easy choice, right?"

"No," I said. "It's not."

"Why not?"

I sighed again. "Don't you see? My Mom wants me to quit. My Dad wants me to play. So if I choose to quit, I'm picking my Mom over my Dad. But if I choose to play, I'm picking my Dad over my Mom."

"I don't think—"

"They're already getting a divorce. Now one of them is going to have hurt feelings. Or be mad at me. Or both."

"Oh." Jill thought about it for a second, then shook her head. "Wait a minute. Are saying that you're *actually* thinking of quitting hockey?"

I didn't answer.

"*Quitting*, Sam? For reals?"

I shrugged. "That's what my Mom wants."

"What about your team?" Jill asked. "And the coaches?"

"Well—"

"What about me?"

"I just—"

"You just want to let us all down?"

"No, I -"

"You can't quit," she said Alexantly.

That warm, fiery feeling started to stir in my stomach again. She didn't understand. This wasn't about whether I wanted to quit or not. How could I pick my Mom over my Dad? Over pick my Dad over my Mom? I needed her help to figure this out.

"I don't know what to do," I started to say, but she interrupted me again.

"Well, it should be obvious," Jill snapped. "But I guess you're just too stupid to see it."

I gaped at her. "Stupid?"

"Stupid," she repeated. "And you're being a selfish jerk," she finished, then turned and walked away.

I stared after her. Anger washed up and down my body. I wanted to yell at her, tell her how she must not be my real friend, how she should just shut up herself because she was stupid and she was the one being a jerk. Most of all, I wanted to tell her she wasn't being fair. But the anger brewing in my stomach felt like it wanted to explode and for some reason I just didn't want to unleash it on Jill.

So I just stood there, watching her braid jump and dance until she went around the corner.

Then I turned to go the other direction and bumped into Nate Bridger.

Literally.

15

I bounced off of Nate Bridger's chest like a puck coming off a goaltender's leg pads. The force of the rebound knocked me back two whole steps.

Nate crossed his arms and tilted back his head. He looked down his nose at me. "Watch where you're walking, *Spam.*"

I clenched my teeth. "I didn't see you," I said.

Nate uncrossed his arms and held them open wide. "Well, I was right here, out in the open for everyone to see." He leaned forward with a sneer. "But that was kinda like that last game we played, wasn't it? You didn't see me then, either, did you?"

Anger roiled in my stomach and climbed up into my chest like flickering flames.

A few kids seemed to sense that something was going on and drifted over toward us.

Nate noticed the beginnings of an audience. He looked back at me and let out a little laugh. "I knew I pasted you good. But I didn't know how good until I heard your coach benched you for being a scaredy cat."

I narrowed my eyes at him. "Where'd you hear that?"

A small crowd gathered nearby. Nate pretended not to notice, but he spoke even louder than normal so that the assembled kids could hear.

"Everyone knows about it," Nate said. "The whole league knows that Sam Parker is a creampuff." He motioned after Jill. "Even your little girlfriend knows it. That's probably why you guys had your little lover's fight."

The warm sensation in my chest burst like a raging forest fire. It spread over my entire body, out to the ends of my arms and legs. My face flushed with warmth. It didn't exactly feel good, but in that moment, I wasn't worried about Jill or hockey or my parents getting a divorce. All I was worried about was balling up my right fist as tight as I could and hurling it toward Nate Bridger's face like I was Dave "The Hammer" Schultz.

My knuckles landed square into his nose. There was something between a smacking and a squishing sound. Blood erupted from both nostrils.

Nate gave me the most surprised look I've ever seen on anyone's face outside of a cartoon. His hands flew to his nose. He let out grunt that had a little bit of a whine in it, as if he didn't know whether to yell or cry. Blood poured through his fingers and dripped onto his white T-shirt that had a picture of a professional wrestler on it.

I waited, unsure what was going to happen next. I could sense the crowd waiting and watching, too. Then Nate turned around and ran toward the building in same direction Jill had gone, holding his nose.

I watched him go. Then I looked down at my hand. It was still balled up in a fist. A small smear of Nate's blood was there between the first and second knuckle.

"Jeez, Sam," someone in the crowd said just loud enough for me to hear. "What got into you?"

I shook my head.

I didn't know.

16

I would have thought that sitting outside the principal's office wouldn't seem like too big of a deal after getting called into the coach's office. Once I was seated outside the big brown door, though, I started to reconsider.

Earlier, Nate Bridger exited the room, holding an icepack to his nose and carrying a blood-stained towel. He gave me a look of cautious resentment before leaving the office area. I wondered what would happen next time we crossed paths.

After Nate left the office, Principal Jenkins called me into her office. She started in on me about how fighting was inappropriate. She didn't even ask why I hit Nate or if Nate started the whole thing.

Finally, she said, "I'm afraid you're going to be suspended for three days."

Suspended?

"But—"

"The school rules are pretty clear on these matters," Principal Jenkins said. "Fighting is an automatic suspension."

"That's not fair," I said.

"How isn't it fair?" she asked calmly.

How? It wasn't fair because Nate Bridger started the fight. It wasn't fair because I've never been in a fight before. In fact, I've never even been in the principal's office for *anything*. It wasn't fair because I had enough to worry about already. I didn't need this, too.

I opened my mouth to say all of that, but all that came out was, "It just isn't."

Principal Jenkins shook her head. "You can't solve problems with your fists, Sam. It just doesn't work. Now, I know that sometimes happens in your hockey games, but—"

"You don't know anything about hockey!" I said to her.

"I know what I see on television," she said, still calm. "And that's not how we solve problems here at school."

I sat in the chair and seethed. She returned my stare for a few moments. Then she said, "I can see you're still angry. Why don't you wait outside until your mother gets here to pick you up, all right?"

I stood up without a word. I left her office without a word. I even slammed the door behind me. A little.

I sat back down outside Principal Jenkins office. When my mom arrived, she gave me a concerned look, patted my hand and went inside. I'm sure that Principal Jenkins told her everything, including how evil she obviously thought hockey was. I wondered what her favorite sport was. Badminton, probably.

I sighed and waited. I stared at the pictures of all the teachers on the wall. Except for Miss Harding and Mr. Zimmerman who were new this year, all of the pictures looked about a hundred years old.

Finally, doorknob rattled and Mom stepped out.

"Let's go, Sam," was all she said.

17

I know some kids get yelled at a lot by their parents. They probably don't like it much. I'm sure I wouldn't, either. But sometimes silence is worse. Especially when you know that there are things that are going to be said. Not good things, either. You know that's coming but you don't know exactly when. Or how angry your parents are going to be about those things. Or what the punishment will be.

Waiting for all of that is almost as bad as when it happens. Maybe worse.

I didn't speak on the ride home.

Neither did Mom.

When we got home, I got a drink of water. I milled around the kitchen, sipping from the glass, just in case she decided that it was time. But she just went into the study and started correcting papers, so I knew it wasn't going to happen yet.

She was probably waiting for Dad to come home. Great. They were going to double-team me.

Dad came home at a little after four.

Nothing happened.

I left the room five times to go to the bathroom down the hall, hoping to catch them in a conversation about me. But the house was quiet.

Around five-thirty, Mom called me to dinner. We sat at the table and ate in silence. It was no different than the last several nights, really. Only this time there was one more thing that we weren't talking about piled on top of the heap.

After dinner, I went back upstairs. I tried to play some video games, but I didn't have much interest. I kept crashing my space fighter into asteroids or getting shot by the robot ships. That was no fun.

At about seven-thirty, I heard steps coming up to my room. Someone rapped on my door, then opened it. Both Mom and Dad stepped into my room.

Here it comes.

Dad took a seat at my desk, turning the chair around to face me. Mom sat on the corner of the bed, folding her hands in her lap. There was a long pause. Then Dad started talking.

It's funny, because I thought he was going to yell at me a little. Instead, he just said, "Sam, we both understand that you're angry about some things right now. We know that getting injured in that game was a rough deal and that you're having a frustrating time with that. Most of all, we know that us getting a divorce is a tough thing for you."

I felt a pang in my chest when he mentioned the divorce. Even though I'd been thinking about it non-stop ever since the first time they told me, I can't remember us ever talking about it out loud since then. I swallowed past the lump in my throat.

"I think you know that you can't go around punching kids at school," Dad continued. "Am I right?"

I nodded.

"And we both know that's not the way you normally handle things. You're just frustrated and angry right now. Am I right there, too?"

I nodded again.

"Feeling that way is all right, Sam," Mom said. She reached out and rubbed my shoulder softly. "You just can't react to those feelings by hitting people."

"I know," I muttered.

We were all quiet for a few seconds. Then Dad asked me, "Is there anything else you want to talk about?"

I thought about it for a minute. I had a question I really wanted to ask but it took me a while to get up the guts to say it. Finally, just as it looked like Dad was finished waiting and started to rise, I burst out, "Why are you getting a divorce?"

Dad stopped. He glanced at Mom, then settled back down on the chair.

"Sam," he said, then stopped.

He looked over at Mom.

I looked over at Mom.

Mom looked at Dad, then at me. She opened her mouth to speak.

"Sam," she said, then stopped.

We all sat there looking at each other for about a minute. It was ridiculous.

"It isn't your fault," Mom said quietly.

"No," Dad said. "It has nothing to do with you."

I shook my head. It had *everything* to do with me. They were my parents.

"Sam, honey, sometimes you just have to trust the people that love you," Mom said. "And even though your father and I are going to be living separately, that doesn't change the fact that we both love you."

"Very much," Dad said.

"We'll make this work as best we can," Mom added.

Make it work? I thought. How can a divorce work? Marriages work. Divorces suck.

Mom squeezed my shoulder gently. Dad reached out and patted me on the leg. They both smiled at me. Then they rose to leave.

"Mom? Dad?"

Both of them turned back around and looked at me expectantly.

I swallowed. "What about hockey?"

They exchanged a glance. Dad shrugged at Mom. Mom shrugged back.

"That's up to you, champ," Dad said. "You can go back on the team if you want. Or you can quit. Your choice."

Both them smiled at me before leaving my room.

I stared at the door as it closed behind them. I was glad that I didn't get into bigger trouble for punching Nate Bridger, but things were worse than before. My parents were definitely still getting a divorce. There was nothing I could do about that. And on top of all that, now I had to choose between them.

Do I pick my Dad and stay in hockey?

Or do I quit and choose my Mom?

I fired up my computer and logged on. I clicked on Jill's avatar and sent her an instant message. Then I waited, watching the cursor blink.

She didn't answer.

"Jill, where are you?" I muttered. Why wasn't she answering my IM? Then I glanced at the clock and realized what time it was.

She was at practice.

Great.

A flicker of cold flame lashed against the walls of my stomach.

Practice. That's where I should be.

I shut off the computer and lay back on my bed. I stared up at the swirls I'd memorized last week. They were no answers there.

The truth was, I didn't know where I was going to find the answer.

18

The next day was a Saturday. Saturday was always game day in hockey. The schedule might vary a little bit during the week as to when we practiced or played, but tradition was that Saturday was always a game day.

I looked at my team schedule. The Rockets were slated to play the Ducks at 6 PM.

I sighed. A night game. We only had one or two Saturday night games a season. It was a big deal. The Junior B team, the Spokane Braves, played at 7:30. Our night game was like a warm up game for that. People came to watch just to watch some hockey before the Braves' game started. Sometimes even other coaches and scouts for Bantam teams came to see who they might draft for the elite level Bantam teams. Even though that was still two years away for me, I'd started thinking about how cool it would be to get drafted. Maybe even play for the Braves or the next level up, the Spokane Chiefs. Of course, all of that was in preparation to play in the NHL some day. That was my dream.

Or at least, it *was* my dream.

Before my concussion.

Before my parents decided to get a divorce.

I sighed again. Maybe our only Saturday night game of the year and I was going to miss it.

Life wasn't fair.

I goofed around the house for most of the day. Video games got boring by ten o'clock. I read a book called "Call of the Wild" for a while. It was about a dog having adventures pulling a sled up in Alaska. That got me through until lunch. After that, I stood out in the driveway and took shots with my basketball. It was a cool October day, just enough to let me sweat a little but not enough to get worn out.

Jill used to have an 8-ball that you could ask questions of. Then you shook the ball and turned it over for the answer. I decided to play a game like that with my basketball. I asked a question of the ball. Then I shot until I made it. Once I made it, I stopped and thought of an answer. Then I shot again. If I made that basket, then I figured it was fate giving me the answer. If I missed, I had to come up with a different answer.

Within fifteen minutes, I discovered that I could stop my parents from getting divorced by becoming an astronaut and that Coach Valka would un-bench me if I washed his car five hundred times.

"This game sucks," I said to no one. I lofted another shot. It bounced off the backboard, careened around the rim and away from the basket.

"Of course it sucks. It's not hockey."

I spun around. Jill stood at the end of my driveway. She had her goalie skates over her shoulder. The basketball bounced and rolled toward her feet. She gathered it in with her foot and kicked it up to her free hand. We stared at each other for a few moments. Then she tossed the ball to me lightly.

"Hey," she said.

"Hey," I said back.

"Put your ball away," she said. "And get your skates. Steve from the skate shop called. Coach Valka arranged for all of us to get a free sharpening for tonight's game. I figured you might want to get yours sharpened along with mine."

I opened my mouth to tell her that I might never need to sharpen my skates again if I quit playing hockey. Then I thought better of it and snapped my mouth shut. Instead, I said, "Okay. Wait here."

I went inside, put away the basketball and got my skates out of my hockey bag. I told Mom where I was going. I expected her to frown or get upset because she thought that meant I was picking Dad instead of her, but she just said it was all right and to be careful crossing Addison, which is a busy street.

Jill and I walked down the street toward Eagles Ice-A-Rena. We didn't speak for several blocks. It was a good silence, though, the kind we'd always had in the past. I didn't know for sure if she was still mad at me or not, but she sure didn't show it.

"Night game today," Jill finally said.

"Yeah, I know."

"You still quitting?"

"I never said I was quitting. I just said I had to pick between what my dad wanted and what my mom wanted."

"I thought about that," Jill answered. "And you know what I think is more important?"

"No," I answered. What could be more important than what your parents wanted?

"I think what *you* want is the most important thing," Jill said.

I thought about that. I could sort of see her point, but she just didn't understand. "That's easy for you to say. Your folks aren't getting divorced."

She shrugged. "Maybe. But I thought about that divorce thing, too."

"Join the club," I said. "It's *all* I think about."

"Well, I asked my mom about it."

"You asked your *mom*?"

She gave me a puzzled look. "Sure. Why not?"

"I don't know. It's just...I don't know, kind of a funny thing to talk to your mom about."

"Not my mom," Jill said. "I can talk to her about anything."

I didn't know what to say to that, so I just listened.

"Anyway," Jill said, "she told me that when people get divorced, it is never because of the kids."

"Never?"

"Nev-*er*," she emphasized. "In fact, she said that sometimes people stay together when they probably shouldn't just because of the kids."

I thought about that for a second, but eventually I shook my head. "I don't know. That sounds like something a parent would tell a kid just to make them feel better."

"My mom wouldn't do that."

"Maybe not."

Jill sighed. "Even if she did, which she didn't, how could this be your fault?"

"Jill, it could be my fault for a *million* different reasons!"

"Like what?"

I opened my mouth to answer, but she interrupted me.

"Do you get good grades in school?"

"Yeah, kinda. Mostly As and Bs."

"Get into any trouble at school?"

"No, except for punching Nate Bridger."

Jill grinned, but didn't comment on that. Instead, she asked, "Do you get in trouble at home?

Not do your chores? Leave huge messes? Talk back to your parents?"

"No, not really. I mean, sometimes I leave dishes in the living room, but –"

"Small potatoes," Jill said. "Face it, Sam. You're a good kid. You are *not* the reason your parents are getting a divorce." She switched her skates over to her other shoulder. "Besides, my mom said it is *never* because of the kids, and my mom would *never* lie to me."

I gave that some thought. On the one hand, if it were true, it was a weight off my shoulders. "Maybe it really wasn't my fault," I said, trying the words on for size.

"Yup."

"On the other hand," I wondered aloud, "why can't my parents be one of those people who stay together because of the kids?"

Jill shrugged. "I don't know. But at least it's not your fault."

"It's not my fault," I repeated. I liked the sound of that.

We rounded a corner. Eagles Ice-a-Rena was just a block ahead. We walked most of the way in silence. I kept repeating the words *It's not my fault* over and over again in my mind. They sounded good. They made me feel...almost happy.

As we neared the doors to the ice rink, Jill said, "Anyway, I just think you should do what you want to do. Play or quit."

I opened my mouth to reply, but she didn't wait. Instead, she opened the door and went inside.

The ice rink was always cool inside, even in the heat of summer. I followed Jill as she made her way to the skate shop. We passed Mr. McC, the Zamboni driver, as he sat sipping his coffee on his stool at the snack counter. He gave us both a wave and smiled that light smile of his. I always thought Mr. McC's job was, well, it was probably the coolest job there was. He got to hang out at the rink all day and every hour or so, he drove the Zamboni, cleaning the sheet of ice for the next group of skaters. Not only was it a fun job, it was also an important one.

When we entered the skate shop, the owner was helping someone else. Steve stood at the register, leaning forward casually, chuckling with a customer who had his back to us. Jill and I waited patiently. Interrupting Steve when he was with a customer was about the only thing I knew of that irritated him, so we never did. Besides, he never let you wait very long.

True to form, he glanced up and saw us. "Ah, there's the budding goaltender, eh?" he said, winking at Jill. Then he looked at me. "How's the noggin, Sam?" he asked, tapping his own head.

Jeez, I thought. *Does everyone know about my concussion or what?*

"It's better," I told him.

"Good, good," he replied. He held out his hands for our skates. "You need those sharpened?"

"Thanks," Jill said. We both handed our skates to him.

Steve touched the blades with his thumb gingerly and shrugged. "Wouldn't hurt, I suppose." He glanced up. "I'll be back in a few."

He disappeared into a room behind the counter. A moment later, the whine of a motor fired up. A second after that, we could hear the scraping, grinding sound of the skate blade being sharpened.

"I love that sound," the customer at the register said, almost as if he were speaking to himself.

I turned my eyes onto him. He was a little younger than my parents, I figured, but not much. He looked familiar to me, but I couldn't immediately figure out why. He had an athletic build, with short dark hair, closely cropped. His eyes held a distant, dreamy expression and his lips were turned up in a half-smile.

"It always meant that skating was just around the corner," he said.

Then he seemed to notice Jill and I standing there. He looked at both of us and smiled. When he did that, a flood of recognition hit me. I opened my mouth, but Jill beat me to the punch.

"You're Alex Ridley," she said breathlessly. "The hockey player."

"I am." He nodded and held out his hand to her. "And you are?"

Jill shook his hand, still awe-struck. "Jill," she managed to say.

"Glad to meet you, Jill." Alex turned to me and extended his hand. "And you?"

I took his hand, expecting him to crush my hand with his NHL grip, but his squeeze was only firm and friendly. "I'm Sam," I said. Then I added, "I play hockey."

As soon as I said it, I felt stupid. My face flooded with warmth. That was something a five-year-old would say. Not someone who was almost twelve. Not to a real NHL player. Even a retired NHL player.

Jill came to my rescue. Sort of.

"So do I," she added.

Great, I thought. *Now he thinks we're both dorks.*

But Alex didn't miss a beat. "That's great. What position do you play?"

"Center," I said.

"Goalie," said Jill, at the same time.

Alex nodded. "Those are both fun positions. I played forward."

"I know," Jill said, her words spilling out like a machine gun. "You used play for the Spokane Chiefs."

He grinned. "That's right. I played Junior here in Spokane. But I grew up north of here, right near the Canadian border. Are you two on the same team?"

We both nodded. Then I stopped in the middle of my nod. Was I still on the team? I didn't want to lie to the only NHL player I'd ever met, even on accident.

I must have been making a face or something, because Alex noticed me. "Something wrong?" he asked.

I shrugged. I didn't know what to say.

"He had a concussion," Jill offered, "so he's been on the bench."

Alex's expression darkened slightly and he nodded knowingly. "I know what that's like," he said quietly.

I remembered my Internet research on NHL concussions. Alex Ridley's career ended because of post concussion syndrome. A hundred questions were rising in my throat. I swallowed hard and tried to decide which one to ask first. I wanted to know how many concussions he had. Did it hurt worse every time it happened? Were his brains scrambled for good? Did it happen every time you took a hard check? Was he scared to get hit anymore?

What came out was, "I might quit."

Then I felt worse than stupid. Shame flooded over me, and I dropped my eyes.

"That's an option," Alex said. There was no condemnation in his voice, so I looked up. His eyes were warm and understanding. "Taking a hard hit is scary enough, without throwing in something like a concussion."

I swallowed. "Is...is that why you quit the NHL?"

He shook his head. "No. I retired because my doctor and my wife convinced me that it was time. They were both right."

"Were you scared?" I asked in a quiet voice. "To get hit, I mean?"

He smiled slightly. "Sure. Of course. Have you seen the size of some of those guys?"

We all three laughed. Then Alex asked, "Are you guys in Pee Wee yet?"

"Yup," Jill said.

Alex glanced at me. "Are you scared to get hit?"

"Sure," I said. "Of course. Have you seen the size of some of those kids?"

We laughed some more. It felt pretty cool to be standing in the skate shop, joking around with a real NHL player who used to be a Spokane Chief. For a moment or two, I even forgot my problems.

"The thing is," Alex said, "everyone is scared of something at some time or another. One of the things I learned in hockey is that it isn't about whether you're afraid or not. It's about doing it anyway, even though you're scared."

I listened closely, nodding my head at his words.

"I was more scared of retirement than I was of getting my clock cleaned by some big huge guy on the ice," he said. "But it was the right thing to do, so I did it even though I was afraid of the idea. And you know what?"

"What?" Jill and I both asked at the same time.

He smiled. "I survived. And life is pretty good."

I thought about his words. I knew he was talking about hockey, but I found myself thinking about my Mom and Dad splitting up. Was he saying that I could survive that, too? I thought about asking him, but decided not to. It was just too personal.

"I'll tell you something else, though," Alex said. "Whether you decide to quit or keep playing, make sure you do it for the right reasons. I played hockey for the right reasons. And I retired for the right reasons. That's why I can stand here and have no regrets."

We stood in silence for a few seconds. The harsh, metallic buzz of skates against the sharpener ceased. A moment later, Steve emerged from the sharpening room.

"All right," he said, plopping our skates down on the rubber padding atop the counter. "A skater and a goalie, razor sharp."

"Thanks," I said.

"Thanks," Jill said.

We both stood there, not wanting to pick up our skates and leave. Alex smiled at both of us, then reached out and shook Steve's hand. "Gotta go," he said. "I'm meeting my wife for an early dinner, then I'm scouting the Braves game tonight."

"See ya next time, Ridder," Steve said.

Alex reached his hand out toward me. "Nice meeting you, Sam. And good luck, whatever you decide to do."

I shook his hand. "Thanks," I said. I wanted to add 'Ridder' but I didn't. Nicknames were for friends and teammates to use. That was the hockey rule. "I will."

"If you keep playing, I might end up scouting you someday soon," Alex said with a grin. "If you don't mind playing for Spokane, that is."

I was speechless. Alex Ridley *scouting* me? For the Chiefs? That was one step away from the pros. I couldn't believe it was possible. But then again, he just said it. Alex Ridley just said it.

"Okay," was all I could say. I was still too much in shock to feel dumb about that lame reply.

Alex squeezed my hand and released it. Then he shook Jill's hand. "Good luck stopping those pucks, little lady. Maybe you could be the first woman to play for the Chiefs, eh?"

"That'd be great!" Jill smiled as big as the sun.

"Keep working, then," Alex said. "Hard work will get you everywhere." Then he tipped a wink at Steve, who winked back. Then he strode out the door with a wave. I noticed him stop and talk with Mr. McC for a second before he left the rink.

"Wow," Jill said. "Did you hear that? He thinks I could play for the Chiefs!"

"Yeah," I said. His words bounced around inside my head. I noticed Steve watching me, but he didn't say anything. After a few moments, I picked up my skates.

"I'll be right back," I told Jill.

"Where are you going?"

"There's something I have to do," I told her, and I left the skate shop.

19

The door was closed, so I wasn't certain if anyone was there. I reached up tentatively and knocked. A few seconds passed. I was about to walk away when a voice barked out, "Come!"

I took a deep breath and opened the door.

Coach Valka sat at his desk, looking down at a diagram. He held a pencil between his fingers, poised above the paper. When I stepped inside, he looked up at me. His expression did not change.

"Parker," he said. "What can I do for you?"

I cleared my throat. "Uh...well...I..."

Coach Valka waited patiently, his expression neutral.

How do I say this?

I realized that the easiest way was just to say it. I cleared my throat again. "Coach, I'm sorry for the way I acted before. When you benched me."

Coach Valka waited a moment, then nodded his head. "Apology accepted. Anything else?"

I nodded. "Uh, yeah." I swallowed hard, then forged ahead. "I was wondering if I could play tonight."

He looked at me long and hard. I tried to read his expression, but Coach Valka has always been one of those grownups that are impossible to read. I had no idea whether he was going to agree to let me play, kick me off the team or what. I figured that after the way I said I was going to quit and slammed his door, chances were his answer would be no.

Finally, he said, "You feel ready?"

A thrill shot through me. I nodded my head vigorously. Maybe he was going to say yes!

"Head's fine?"

"Feels great," I said.

"What about getting hit?" His eyes bore into me. "I can't have you running from body checks out there."

I shook my head. "I won't," I promised.

Coach Valka continued to look at me. I looked back at him, trying to project as much confidence as I could. Alex Ridley's words filled my head.

It isn't about whether you're afraid or not. It's about doing it anyway, even though you're scared.

I wondered if Coach Valka could sense the change in me. I hoped so.

Finally, he simply said, "Okay. See you at game time, Parker." Then he looked back down at the diagram in front of him.

Elation zinged through me. I sat stock-still for a few seconds, soaking in the thrill. I was back in the game.

I stood to leave. As I turned toward the door, I saw a slip of paper tacked to the small corkboard hanging beside Coach Valka's desk. It was a phone number with a single word on it.

Ridder, it said.

20

I told Jill my decision on the way home. I expected her to be excited, but she just shrugged.

"Of course you're going to play," she said. "You're a hockey player, Sam."

We walked for a while longer in silence. Then I heard Jill let out a long breath. I looked over and a huge smile was busting out of her face.

"What's so funny?" I asked her.

She looked at me like I was dense. "We got to meet Alex Ridley," she said in awestruck tones.

"I know."

"Isn't that the coolest thing *ever*?"

I smiled. It was pretty cool.

We walked the rest of the way to my house, then Jill continued on. I walked inside and put my skates away. Then I checked in the kitchen for my Mom. She wasn't there, or in the study. I knocked on the bedroom door, but there was no answer. Dad was nowhere to be found, either. Finally, I wandered out into the back yard. Mom sat on grass. She had her head tilted back to catch the sun. Her eyes were closed, but when I sat down beside her, she opened them a slit and squinted at me.

"How are you feeling, honey?" she asked.

"Really good," I said.

She smiled and closed her eyes again. The sun was warm but a slight breeze kept it from feeling too hot. It was pretty much a perfect day, in fact.

"Last of the Fall sun, I think," she said quietly.

I looked at my Mom in the sunlight. She looked a little bit more tired than normal, and I noticed lines in her face that I hadn't seen there before. Still, at that moment, with the sun shining down on her, she looked happy.

Which made what I was about to say even harder to get off my chest.

"Uh, Mom?"

"Mmmmm?"

"I talked with Coach Valka."

"When?" she asked, her eyes still closed.

"Today," I said. "At the rink. When I got my skates sharpened."

She nodded and said nothing. I imagined that I saw a little bit of a tightening around the corners of her mouth, but I could have been wrong.

"Anyway," I pressed on, talking over the lump in my throat. "He said he would play me tonight. So, uh, I'm...I'm going to play."

There it was. Now she knew what my choice was. I waited for her to react. My stomach was clenched in icy knots as I hoped she didn't think that because I wanted to play that I was choosing Dad over her. I didn't want to hurt her feelings or make her think I didn't love her. I didn't want to ruin the last of her Fall sunshine, either. But there was nothing I could do except tell her what my decision was and wait.

She didn't say anything for a full minute. She just sat there, the sun on her face, her eyes closed. Then she smiled up into the sun, tilted her head toward me and opened her eyes the tiniest bit. "Okay, honey," she said. "If that's what you'd like to do, it's all right with me."

Relief washed over me. "Really?" I asked.

"Of course," she said. "I just want you to be happy."

Wow, I thought. And I figured she'd be upset.

"Sam?" she asked me. "Just one thing, okay?"

"Sure, Mom. What's that?"

Mom laid back on the grass. She put her hands behind her head and squinted at me. "I think what they say is, 'keep your head up,' right?"

I smiled. "You bet."

I laid down next to her. We lay soaking in the sun and watching the clouds pass by. For a while, everything was all right in the world.

21

Electricity buzzed through the locker room. Everyone seemed pumped up for the Saturday night game. I sensed it as soon as I came through the door and found a place to sit and change. I also sensed a few doubtful looks from some of my teammates.

I knew what they were thinking. They weren't sure they could count on me.

They were afraid I was going to let them down.

So was I, to be honest.

I didn't say a word, though. I knew that nothing I could say would do anything to change their fears. I'd have to let my actions on the ice speak for me.

Coach Andy came in while I was lacing up my skates. He didn't say a word, but he gave me a smile and squeezed my shoulder. I smiled back and finished tying my skate.

When Coach Valka came in, the excitement had reached a steady pitch. Usually he had a calming effect on the team, but tonight it seemed like he amplified our excitement.

"Are you boys ready for some hockey?" he asked in his gravelly voice.

"Yes!"

"What's that?"

"YES, COACH!"

I thought I saw a flicker of a smile at the corner of Coach Valka's mouth. "Good," he said. "Here are the lines."

He rattled off names. I was surprised when he said my name because he still had me on the first line. I thought he might put me on the second line after everything that happened, but he didn't. That could only mean one thing – Coach Valka believed in me.

I felt my chest swell up just a little, in spite of my worry about the coming game.

When the lines were finished, Coach Valka said, "This might be a big game, since it's a Saturday night tilt. But just remember – it's the same game on the same ice as every other game you've played. So let's not forget how to play just because of what time it is."

Several players nodded their understanding.

"Play hard," Coach Valka said. "Play smart. And play together. Understand?"

"YES, COACH!"

He turned to Coach Andy. "Anything?"

Coach Andy smiled. "Just one thing. Anyone know what it is?"

"Have fun!" we all yelled back at him.

His smile spread across his face. "That's right."

Have fun? I thought. I was too scared to have fun.

"All right, then," Coach Valka said. He nodded toward Jill. "Lead us out."

As soon as we hit the ice, the butterflies started. I felt like I had a swarm of cold razor blades in my stomach, slicing and battering the walls of my gut.

Down at the other end of the ice, the opposing team was already skating warm-ups. Their green uniforms zipped through the drill.

The Ducks.

Of course.

I turned away before I succumbed to the temptation to look for Nate Bridger. I was pretty sure I'd be seeing him soon enough.

My legs were shaky as Coach Andy put us through a quick skate and then had us shoot pucks on net. Jill stopped almost every shot with authoritative technique. She oozed confidence in the crease. I wished I'd asked her how she managed that. I could have used some.

"Pucks in," hollered the referee.

I flicked a few pucks lightly toward our bench, where Coach Andy gathered them into the puck bag. Then we congregated at the bench.

"Play your game," Coach Valka said simply.

We put our gloves in and chanted "Rockets!" in one voice. Then I turned and glided toward center ice. My stomach was a whirling mess. My heart pounded like a hammer in my chest. I tried to swallow, but my mouth was dry.

I skated to a stop at the face-off dot, looking at the skates of the opposing center. I knew who it was going to be before I ever looked up.

"I don't believe it," Nate Bridger said. "It's Spam."

I looked up into his eyes. Even behind the cage of his facemask, I could see that the area around both of his eyes were bruised a deep blue. I felt a little bit bad about that, so I said, "I'm sorry I punched you."

"Oh, you will be," Nate said. "One cheap shot deserves another."

Before I could answer, the referee skated to center ice. He checked with both goalies and the timekeeper, then he dropped the puck and it was game on.

Just like before, Nate didn't bother going for the puck. As soon as the puck left the referee's hand, he charged right into me. His shoulder slammed into my head. The force of the hit sent me sprawling on the ice.

It hurt.

Actually, it hurt a *lot*.

My head was spinning from the force of the blow. I half-expected to hear a whistle because it was illegal to check a player in the head. Play continued around me, though, so I guessed that the referee didn't see it.

I didn't want to get up.

I didn't want to get hit like that again and again. Fear washed over me like a tidal wave. It seemed like I lay there forever. I imagined that the whistle would blow at any moment, this time because the ref saw me and thought I was injured. Not just too afraid to get up.

It isn't about whether you're afraid or not. It's about doing it anyway, even though you're scared.

I shook the cobwebs from my head and scrambled back to my feet.

22

I skated back into the play. My legs were weak, but I forced the strides that got me across the ice and into our zone.

The Ducks moved the puck from player to player. Their passes always seemed to be a second ahead of our reaction to the play. The defenseman had their forwards covered down in front of the crease. Jill moved from side to side, tracking the puck as it zipped from player to player. Our forwards remained high in the zone, trying to cover their defenseman.

Nate Bridger was all alone in the slot. He stood between the two circles at the hash marks, just a few feet outside the crease, with his stick on the ice, in prime scoring position.

He was wide open.

And that was my man. I was supposed to be covering him.

I lowered my head and skated hard.

Nate tapped his stick on the ice, calling for the puck. I looked up at him, expecting to see him glaring at me, waiting for another chance to blast into me. Instead, he was looking off to the defenseman on the right wing, anticipating a pass.

I glanced over to my right just in time to see the defenseman send the puck in Nate's direction. I lowered my shoulder. Just as the puck arrived, I drove my shoulder as hard as I could into Nate Bridger's chest.

If this had been a movie or something, I think that the force of my check would have sent him sprawling. The crowd would have cheered and the tide of the game would have swung our direction.

But this wasn't a movie. It was real life.

I bounced off of Nate like a superball and fell over backwards. I landed with a hard smack on the ice. Most of my breath swooshed out, but I didn't quite suffer the full meal deal of getting the wind knocked out me. Even so, I lay still for a second before I rolled over onto my belly and rose slowly to my feet.

A few feet away, Nate Bridger was getting up, too.

It took me a second to realize what that meant.

I knocked him down.

I knocked down Nate Bridger.

He got to his skates and strode away, back toward the puck. As he passed by, he gave me a strange look, a mixture of confusion and anger.

I actually smiled.

One of our players must have taken possession and moved the play out of our zone, because there was a mob of skaters battling for the puck over on the boards in the neutral zone. I started that way, still amazed at what had happened.

The ref blew the play dead and both coaches called for a line change. I skated to the bench. My arms and legs were alive and tingling with energy. Even after I sat down, the sensation continued.

Coach Valka dropped his hand on my shoulder. "Nice hit, Parker. Good defensive play."

My chest swelled with pride. Coach Valka didn't hand out compliments like candy at Halloween. You had to earn them.

I watched the game from the bench. The Ducks kept control of the puck and moved it into our zone. The forward carried the puck down into the corner. Both of our defensemen peeled off to go after him. That left the other forward open in front of the net. The puck-carrier made a hard pass across the ice, right onto the tape of the forward's stick. All he had to do was make a sweeping motion and he buried the puck into the yawning net. Jill had no chance.

"That's okay," Coach Andy said. "Let's get it back!"

Coach Valka changed the lines. I met Nate Bridger at center ice for the faceoff.

"Bet you wouldn't try that cheap stuff when I'm looking, Spam," he sneered at me.

"We'll see," I said.

The referee dropped the puck. I drove toward Nate. He drove toward me. We collided. I bounced backward. So did he, though not as far as I did. We stared at each other for second, then the ref said, "Play the puck!"

I slipped to the side, tapping the puck past Nate. He yelled in surprise and flipped around to pursue me. I turned on the jets and carried the puck into the offensive zone. As their defenseman closed on me, I snapped the puck toward the net. For a moment, I was sure the puck would slip past their goalie and the red light would go on. Instead, I heard the sound of hard rubber against a stick blade and saw the puck bouncing toward the corner.

The Ducks gathered in the puck and started up ice with it. I fell back defensively, keeping any eye on Nate and the two forwards. The left wing was a smallish kid with lots of speed and that was who the defenseman decided to pass to. Our defenseman on that side was big, but not quite fast enough, so the winger slipped past him with the puck.

I pulled away from net and toward the puck carrier.

"Three on two!" bellowed Coach Valka from the bench, letting us know that they had three skaters coming into our zone against only two of us. I knew right away from all of our drills that my job was to stop the shooter from making a pass to either of the other two players. Force him to shoot and let the goalie stop the shot.

I angled my stick in the passing lane, gliding backward. The shooter didn't even look to his right. Instead, he wound up for a slap shot. I shifted my stick to the shooting lane, hoping to deflect his shot wide. At the last second, he dropped his stick to the puck and rocketed a pass toward the middle of the ice. I lashed out at it with my stick, but it was too late.

Nate Bridger was right there in the slot, just like before. He didn't even stop the pass before he shot it. Instead, he one-timed it, shooting the puck as soon as it arrived. His shot blasted past Jill and into the back of the net for a goal.

2-0.

The Ducks cheered. We skated dejectedly back to the bench.

"No worries," Coach Andy said. "There's a whole lot of hockey left."

"Just play tight to the body," Coach Valka told us. "Make them battle through checks."

I took a drink of water and looked down at my skates.

On the next shift, I rammed into Nate as hard as I could. We both went sprawling on the ice again. The force of the collision shook my whole body, but I got right back up and skated after the puck. I resisted the temptation to say anything to Nate about it. All he'd have to do is point up at the scoreboard, anyway.

Later in the shift, Jill made a glove save and the whistle blew. Coach Valka called a line change. As I skated to the bench, I looked up into the stands and found my Mom sitting where they usually sat.

They.

I realized that I wasn't going to be able to say "they" anymore. That brought a lump up from my stomach, through my chest and into my throat. I swallowed past it and looked for my Dad. He was nowhere to be seen.

I wondered if that was how it was going to be now. Would only one of them come to my games at a time?

I shook my head and stepped off the ice.

The first period ended, but the second period was more of the same. The Ducks kept the pressure on and we couldn't seem to get anything going. Jill made some great saves to keep us in the game. Every time I stepped on the ice, I tried to lay a hit on Nate, but I didn't always get the chance. He got me a couple of times, too, catching me down in the corner as I was trying to dig the puck out from between the legs of a Ducks defenseman.

Every time I got on the ice, a surge of fear rumbled through my belly.

Every time I felt that, I just reminded myself what Alex told me.

It isn't about whether you're afraid or not. It's about doing it anyway, even though you're scared.

I did it anyway. Sometimes, Nate did it to me.

It hurt. Sometimes it hurt a lot. But Alex was right.

I survived.

23

The second period ended with the Ducks still leading 2-0. When I skated out for the third period faceoff, I glanced up at my Mom. That's when I saw my Dad sitting next to her. Both of them noticed me looking at the same time and waved at me. For one short, sweet moment, I imagined that him sitting there somehow meant that they were back together. A second later, I realized how baby-ish that thought was.

All eyes were on me, since we were about to take the faceoff. I couldn't wave back like some Junior Mite player waving to Mommy and Daddy, so I settled for a nod.

The ref dropped the puck and Nate and I slammed together, battling for possession.

That's how the period went. One collision at a time. One battle at a time. I tried to use my speed to break free, but the Ducks stuck to me like glue. Nate bodied up on me every chance he got.

Coach Valka always said that the clock was a fickle thing. When you're ahead, it seems to slow, taking forever to tick off the seconds until you get the victory. When you're behind, it flows like water, ripping through the seconds until you're simply out of time.

That's what seemed to be happening. Every time I glanced up at the clock, the red numbers seemed to be taunting us all, flitting by at light speed. Our league played fifteen minute periods, but it seemed like only a minute passed and we were down to ten. Two shifts and one teeth-rattling check from a Ducks defenseman who was even bigger than Nate later, the clock read 5:21. We held the line defensively and when we didn't, Jill came up with a good save. We just couldn't score.

With 2:44 left in the game, Carson flipped a weak shot toward their goalie, who gloved it and stopped play. Coach Valka sent my line out. I won the draw straight back to the defenseman, who wasted no time in shooting the puck. The shot was low. The goalie dropped to his knees, butterflying out the large leg pads and planting the stick down firmly on the ice. The puck rebounded off the thick pads with a resounding thump. I took one huge stride that direction, reached out and flicked the puck toward the top of the net before Nate or the defenseman could stop me.

The goalie grasped at the puck as it sailed past him and into the netting for a goal.

Our side of the ice exploded with cheering. My teammates on the bench hooted and hollered and banged their sticks against the boards. My linemates surrounded me, tapping my helmet with their gloves.

"Oh yeah!"

"Nice shot!"

"Way to go, Sam!"

We skated back toward center ice for the face off. I looked over at my parents. Both of them were clapping and smiling. Mom gave me an excited wave. Dad flashed me a thumbs up. I raised my stick back toward them.

Them, I thought.

I guess *they* were still *them*.

Kinda.

I didn't have time to work on that, because Coach Valka called for a timeout.

At the bench, he took the time to give me an appreciative nod, then turned his attention to the dry erase board. "When we get possession of the puck, let's get it into their zone," he said, scratching some Xs on the board. He pointed at Jill. "That's when you come to the bench for the extra skater. Wait for me to wave for you."

Jill nodded. "Okay, Coach."

Coach Valka added an extra X on the board, then pointed at Carson. "You're our extra man," he told the center. He looked across the group of assembled skaters. "We need to outnumber them on the puck. Get possession. Get a shot and crash the net. We only need one goal to tie it up here."

We put our hands in and gave a loud "Rockets!" chant before heading back to center ice for the faceoff. Nate was there waiting for me.

"Don't even think about being a hero, Spam," he growled at me.

I didn't answer.

The referee blew his whistle and dropped the puck.

Nate slammed into me like a monster truck. I flew backward, landing on my backside and sliding along the ice. My whole world shook for a few seconds. During that time, I watched Nate grab the puck and skate forward with it.

I shook my head to clear it. I was rewarded with a small gong of pain on each shake. Ignoring that, I rolled over onto my knees. Nate was close, about to skate right past me, where he'd have a great shot on goal. I had to stop him. I leaned forward and stabbed at the puck with my stick.

Nate seemed to know what I was planning to do before I did. He pulled the puck to his left, out of my reach, and kept going past me.

I clenched my jaw and hopped to my feet. Maybe I could catch up to him before he got off a shot. I lowered my head and skated hard. When I looked up, Nate was winding up for a slapshot. I dove forward at the puck, leaning forward with my stick. It didn't have to be perfect, just enough to stymie his shot.

Nate's stick came down and blasted the puck a second before I got there. The shot rocketed toward Jill as I slid harmlessly past Nate on my belly.

Jill's glove hand flashed out. She snagged the puck in the webbing of her glove and pulled the glove to her chest.

A cheer rose from our side of the ice.

Nate swung his stick downward, smacking it on the ice in frustration.

Everyone seemed to slow down, expecting a whistle. Before that could happen, though, Jill flipped the puck to the side of the net and onto one of the surprised defenseman's stick.

"Keep it moving!" she hollered at him.

I hopped to my feet. The clock read 1:56 and counting. I circled slightly to pick up speed and started up ice. The defenseman recovered his wits and hit me with a pass just as I flew by Nate, who was still at a stand-still.

"Hey!" he yelled after me.

I shot up the ice, pushing the puck out in front of me. As I approached their blue line, both defenseman converged on me, so I hurled the puck past them and into the corner of the offensive zone. One defenseman broke away to pursue the puck. The other tried to line me up for a hit. I cut back hard and he slid right past me.

I went after the puck in the corner.

The Ducks defenseman got there first. He bobbled it, trying to get control on the rough third period ice. I lowered my shoulder and barreled right into him, catching him square in the chest and stapling him to the boards.

I bounced back from the check while the defenseman seemed momentarily frozen. I reached between his skates with the blade of my stick and fished out the puck. Then I turned slightly up-ice, looking for a teammate to pass it to.

That's when the freight train named Nate Bridger plowed into me.

His weight crushed me into the boards, knocking the breath out of me. My whole body shook and a heavy pain bounced and ricocheted through me.

And then it was over.

I didn't even fall down.

Before I could think, I reached for the puck again. I didn't know where anyone was, and didn't have time to look, so I played it safe and sent the puck deeper into the zone.

"Empty net!" came the call from the Ducks bench. Some of their fans took up the cry.

Nate pushed off of me and went after the puck.

I went after Nate.

Down below the net, one of our forwards battled for the puck with one of the Ducks defensemen. Nate arrived and used his hips to push my line mate away from the puck. I lowered my shoulder and drove into Nate. He grunted and budged a little, but kept his stick near the puck.

It became a free for all as we jabbed and swept at the puck, trying to get control. Nate switched from bumping and grinding against the other winger to directing his energy toward me. I slid my skate in between the puck and his stick, giving me a free shot at grabbing the biscuit. Just as I got it on my stick blade, all those jamming and jabbing sticks pushed my skate out from under me. I fell to my knees.

Out of the corner of my eye, I saw Carson streaking up the slot toward the net. I spun away from Nate and the other players and zipped a pass right to him.

Carson one-timed the shot.

The goalie flailed at it with his stick but missed.

Tink!

The puck struck the pipe and bounced back out. It landed near one of the Ducks, who blindly flung the puck back up the ice and out of the zone.

I let out a deep breath and glanced at the clock. Forty-three seconds left. We still had a chance. The Ducks player had shot the puck from his own side of the red line, so it would be an icing call. That meant the clock would stop and we'd have a faceoff down at this end of the ice. With six players against their five, hopefully we could get the tying goal.

The crowd started to rumble excitedly. They excitement quickly built. Spectators leaned forward, looking down at our end of the ice.

I followed their gaze just in time to see the puck glide into our empty net for a goal.

24

The Ducks bench and their fans exploded into cheers.

The score flipped to three on their side. I shook my head in disbelief. We skated toward the bench, our morale broken. Coach Valka waved us back to center ice, except for Carson, who returned to the bench. Jill made the lonely skate back to her crease.

The referee dropped the puck. The Ducks bench and their fans cheered continuously for the last thirty seconds of the game. When the clock reached ten seconds, they all counted down. When the buzzer sounded, they broke into an even louder cheer. The players left the bench and mobbed their goalie while we milled around the bench, watching.

"Hold your heads high," Coach Valka told us, no trace of disappointment in his voice. "Now go congratulate your goaltender. She played one heck of a good game."

I skated toward Jill, who was already waiting at the blue line.

"Great saves," I told her.

"Nice try at the end," she said.

We went through the handshake line with the Ducks. Every player said an exuberant "Good Game!" which was a lot easier to say for them, since they won. Still, I did like Coach Valka said and held my head high.

When I reached Nate, he squeezed my hand hard, making my fingers hurt. "Better luck next time, Spam," he said derisively.

"Good game," I said back, ignoring what a jerk he was.

We made our way into the locker room. Once everyone was there, Coach Valka entered. He looked around the room at all of us. Finally, he said, "Every time I step out onto that ice with a team, I expect to win. I strive to win. That is what we work hard in practice to do. To win." He continued to scan the players in the room. "But the reality is that we are not going to win every game. When those times happen, you have to ask yourself if you gave everything you had out there. If you did, then there's nothing more to do except learn what you can from the loss and prepare for the next game. Because no one wins every game. Not in hockey, and not in life."

His eyes came to rest on me.

"I'm proud of each and every one of you today," he said.

"So am I," said Coach Andy.

25

After the game, I rode home with Dad. Mom followed in her car. She'd asked me if it hurt all the times I got hit during the game. Her face had a slightly pinched look of worry on it when she asked. I didn't want to lie to her, but I didn't want to worry her, either.

"A little, but not much," I settled on saying.

On the ride home, Dad and I were quiet for a while. Every so often, he made an observation about the game, then we fell silent again.

"That was a great goal, Sam," he told me.

"Thanks," I said.

Silence.

"Good effort there at the end. I thought Carson had that one for sure."

"Yeah," I said.

More silence.

He cleared his throat. "You guys have nothing to be ashamed of," he said.

"I know," I answered. "Coach Valka told us."

"Good," he said.

Silence.

When we reached the house, Mom pulled her car into the garage, but Dad stopped his car in the driveway. I didn't ask why. I figured he was going to take off somewhere, just like he did after practice that time.

Instead, he turned off the engine. Then he turned to me. "Sam, I'm sorry I missed the first period of your game."

"It's okay," I said.

He shook his head. "No, it's not. Things like that are important. I wanted to be there. I just got tied up with something that took longer than I thought."

"It's okay," I repeated.

He smiled and ruffled my hair. "You're a great kid, you know?"

I shrugged, but his words felt good.

We sat in silence for a few more seconds, then Dad said, "The thing is, the reason I was late? I was signing some paperwork for an apartment."

I furrowed my brow. "An apartment?"

He nodded. "Yes. I was signing a lease. I'm moving out of the house and into an apartment."

I stared at him. "You're leaving us?"

He shook his head. "No, Sam. I'm just moving into an apartment. You and I will still see each other all of the time. It won't be perfect. It won't be like it was. But it'll be all right."

I wanted to scream at him to change his mind or to make Mom change hers. But somehow I didn't think that would make a difference. Just like I knew it wasn't my fault, I also knew I couldn't do anything to stop it.

"Okay," was all I could think to say.

"Okay?" Dad asked, his eyebrows going up in surprise.

I nodded with more confidence than I felt. "Yeah. It's okay. It'll be okay."

Dad looked at me for a long moment. Then he ruffled my hair again. "Okay then."

We got out of the car and went up the walkway. My feet felt like they were filled with lead. I dragged them along like anchors.

Dad paused at the door, as if deciding whether or not to knock. Instead, he flipped through his mound of keys, searching for the house key. Before he could find it, Mom opened the door for us.

"Thanks," Dad said, looking up.

She nodded. "You're welcome."

She stepped to the side and we walked through the open door. I started toward the kitchen to get a drink when I noticed a suitcase and a smaller leather clothes bag in the entry way.

I stopped. I looked up at my parents. Both were watching me.

"Now?" I asked. "You're leaving *now*?"

Dad nodded. "There will never be a good time, Sam. But now is the time."

I didn't want him to go. He held open his arms to me and I walked toward him. I wrapped my arms around his body and squeezed. He held me tight with one arm. With the other, he patted my head gently.

"It'll be all right, son," he said quietly. "It'll be all right."

The tears came to my eyes unbidden. I choked back some of them, but a few escaped. I squeezed a little harder.

After what seemed like forever, I pulled back and looked up at my Dad. His eyes were glistening, but he smiled down at me. "You're a great kid. I love you, son."

"I love you, too, Dad," I said.

He kissed the top of my head, then ruffled my hair. I let go of him, even though all I wanted to do was keep hanging on until he decided not to leave.

Dad picked up the suitcase in one hand and the bag in the other. He looked at Mom. "I'll call you soon. We'll work out the details."

Mom nodded but said nothing.

Dad looked back at me again. He flashed me a grin. "I'll talk to you tomorrow, champ."

"Okay, Dad." I said.

He turned and walked out the door.

I stood in the doorway and watched as he loaded the bags into the back of his car. As he did so, Jill walked up the sidewalk. When I saw her, I hurriedly wiped away the tears on my face. Jill stopped at his car and talked to him for a moment, then headed up toward the front steps to the porch.

My dad got inside his car, started it up and backed down the driveway. He gave me a little wave as he pulled away.

I watched his car go. Mom put her arm around my shoulders and squeezed. Jill reached out and took my hand. None of us said a word as Dad's car approached the corner. Then he turned and disappeared from view.

I didn't like what was happening at all. In fact, I hated it. I wanted to find a way to run from it or change it. I wanted to make it the way that it used to be, but I knew I couldn't.

Jill and I stepped out of the doorway. Mom closed the door.

"Thirsty?" she asked me.

I nodded. "Parched."

She turned to Jill and raised her eyebrows questioningly. "Jill?"

"Yes, please, Mrs. Parker."

"I'll make some lemonade, then," Mom said. She smiled at me again, then turned to go toward the kitchen. In the entry way, I could still smell my Dad's cologne in the air. I stood there, enjoying the sense of him in that moment. Then I glanced over at Jill. She was smiling at me.

That's when I realized I was still holding her hand. I let go suddenly, a little embarrassed. Jill's expression didn't change. If anything, she smiled bigger, even though a tinge of red showed up on her cheeks.

"You okay?" she asked me.

I figured she meant all of it – the hockey, my parents, and maybe the moment of hand-holding just a second ago. I cleared my throat and nodded my head. "Yeah," I said. "I'm okay."

"You sure?"

I took a deep breath and wiped my eyes again, getting the last of my tears. "I'm sure," I said.

Jill grinned and punched me lightly in the arm. "Good. Because you're my best friend, you know?"

I smiled a little. "Yeah?"

"Yup."

"Well," I said, "you want to go get some food?"

"Yup."

As we headed toward the kitchen, I thought about what Alex Ridley said to both of us about his retirement and how he'd been afraid of it.

I survived, he told us.

Survive?

Well, if he could, I could.

The End

Acknowledgements

Thanks to:

Mrs. Taylor's 2008-09 sixth grade class in Sisters, Oregon, for the first round of great feedback on an early draft.

Fleur Bradley, Jill Maser and Dawn Richard for reading the first draft and making it better.

The 2010-11 Spokane Jr. Chiefs Squirt B hockey team (along with Coach Moon), for teaching me numerous things about hockey...and life.

My youngest son, Nico, for giving me constant inspiration and joy on this subject.

My oldest son, Mitchell, for having done the same, years ago.

My wife, Kristi, for helping every step of the way.

About the Author

Frank Scalise has been writing since he was ten years old. He was in the Army and is a police officer. He writes crime fiction under the name Frank Zafiro.

Frank loves to play and watch hockey. His favorite teams are the Spokane Chiefs (WHL) and the Philadelphia Flyers (NHL).

He has two dogs. Richie is named after a hockey player. Wiley has a bull rider named after him.

Made in the USA
Charleston, SC
26 October 2012